A Secret Hood Love Affair

The Princess and JA Story

Written By:

PATRICE BALARK

Copyright

A Secret Hood Love Affair

Copyright © Patrice Balark

Published By: Cole Hart Signature Novels

Publishers Note

Published by Cole Hart Presents

First Quarter

PRINCESS

2005

I'm lookin' for Mrs. Bubble Gum
I'm Mr. Chik-O-Stick
I wanna (dun dun dunt) (oh)
Cause you so thick
Girls call me Jolly Rancher
Cause I stay so hard
You can suck me for a long time
(Oh my God!)

"It's hot as fuck out here," Courtney said, fanning herself with her right hand while her oversized Chanel shades covered damn near half her face.

"Well, bitch, it wouldn't be so hot if you got yo' bougie ass in the pool," I shot back, while I sat alongside my cousin at the local community pool center.

"Girl, bye. These ghetto-ass kids pissing, slobbing, oh, and look at them over there, they damn near fucking in this pool. No, thank you. I rather stay STD free and sit pretty over here," she replied, turning up her nose at everybody who walked past.

I looked at Courtney's ass and laughed. My favorite cousin was a mess, a hot mess, but that was how she was raised. That was actually how both of us were raised. Our fathers, Quincy and Quintin, known to the drug world as "The Taylor Twins", ran a lucrative cartel right here in Chicago, but they were not to blame for my cousin's stuck-up ways; it was our mothers, Tamika and Dominique.

I am the only child belonging to Tamika and Quincy. There was no high school sweethearts, teenage love story to tell. My dad fucked, got her popped, and being the smart woman my mother was, she stuck around, and now she was one of the richest women in the Mid-West. About a year later, clearly not learning from his brother's mistakes, my Uncle Quintin did the same thing with Auntie Domo, and wallah, here came Courtney's black ass.

Courtney and I had grown up super close, and we lived in the same neighborhood, right across the street from each other. Our family had bought all the homes on that block, had the shit sectioned off with gates, and called it an estate. When you give black people money, they create their own shit. I wasn't mad though because I had a sister, minus having to share, so I was good.

"Girl, look, here come yo' boo," Courtney said, popping her gum.

"I ain't thinking about Pierre. He can keep his ass over there," I replied, now flipping my shades down from off the top of my head.

I watched my sixteen-year-old boyfriend bypass all the groupies as they broke their necks trying to speak to him. About a minute later, all the paparazzi disbursed, and he stood behind me, tapping me on the shoulder.

"What's up!" I said, tilting my glasses off my eyes, resting them on the bridge of my nose.

"Don't start acting crazy, Princess," he replied.

"Naw, I'm straight. I'm gone always be straight, remember that," I spat, rolling my eyes and placing the Gucci sunglasses back on.

"Yo, what's yo' cousin's problem, Courtney?" Pierre asked, taking a seat next to me on the side of the pool.

"Boy, you are her problem. First of all, you ain't call her back last night, then we heard about how this morning you went to IHOP with Stephanie's old tired, stiff weave wearing ass."

Although I was playing the mad role, I couldn't help but laugh.

"I fell asleep last night, once I put my phone on the charger, and I went to IHOP with the team; Stephanie and nem just so happened to be there," he responded.

"Oh, really? Well, how about I ask her myself, here she come now," I said, taking my feet out the pool.

I walked over in the direction of Stephanie and her friends as they stood off by the lifeguard post. She noticed me coming first, and I noticed her nudge her friends with her elbow.

"Yo, I got a question," I said, stepping to them.

"What's up?" she said, smiling hard as fuck.

"This morning, IHOP, did you go with Pierre?" I asked, getting straight to the point.

Stephanie looked at me, then at her two friends before they all started laughing hysterically.

Calm down, Princess. Count to ten. One...two...three...four...five...

The more I tried to calm myself down, the louder they laughed, which only made my anger grow.

Six...seven...eight...nine...

But before I could make it to ten, I swung on Stephanie. I beat her ass while the other two Stooges stood back and watched their fearless leader get whooped. I threw her around like a rag-doll while everybody at the pool watched.

"Why are you over here fighting?" I heard Courtney say as she stood on the side of me, stomping Stephanie.

This damn fool had her nerve, but this had become a regular thing of ours. You see, bitches tried us left and right. They thought because we came from money, we were some hoes. They saw all this designer shit and thought we were just some weak, rich bitches, but if they knew better, they'd do better. We came from a family full of killers.

"PRINCESS, STOPPPP!" Pierre yelled, pulling me off Stephanie while Courtney got one last kick to the face.

"FINISH HERRRR!" I yelled as Pierre pulled me out of the gate, away from all the commotion.

"Yo, what the fuck is wrong with you? Why you can't control your temper? One minute you cool, and the next, you spazzing. Princess, you need to be easy!" he yelled.

"Disrespect. I don't take disrespect very well, and you know that," I said in my defense.

"You went over there fucking with them, though," he said, calmer than before.

"Man, whatever, I'm finna go," I responded, waiting for Courtney to make it over to me.

"Why must we fight everywhere we go, Princess?" she asked, out of breath.

"Courtney, don't even start. I just asked her crazy ass the same thing," Pierre said.

"What, she hit you with the *'I don't take disrespect very well'* line?" Courtney said, mocking me.

"Hell yeah," Pierre agreed as they laughed.

And that was my cue to walk off. I was already mad, and I didn't need to be out there fighting my so-called boyfriend and cousin because their asses were next. As soon as I turned around, I was greeted by Stephanie and a glass bottle that went upside my head. After that, I remember going to the hospital and finding out some news that would change my life, for the rest of my life.

2016 (Present day)

"Mommy, are we going to the mall or nah?"

I looked up from my phone at my ten-year-old daughter who flopped down on my bed in a pair of True Religion blue jeans and a pink and white shirt to match.

"Harmony, if you don't get yo' ass out my face," I said, laughing.

"See, mommy, why you play so much? You told me after you got done with your paperwork we were going to go to the mall," she shot back.

"And I'm not done, little girl, so go find you some business."

"Well, per your Facebook status, and I quote, *'I'm so glad I'm done with this paperwork, now I can relax.'* So, mommy, you lying to me or to Facebook?" she asked, dead ass serious.

I couldn't help but laugh. This little girl was me reincarnated, and all the hell I had given my parents growing up, I guess it was payback time.

"A'ight, go put on your shoes, and welcome to the block party, Harmony," I smiled and said as she hopped up and walked towards the door.

She stopped dead in her tracks before turning around and looking at me. "Block party? What you talking about?" she quizzed.

"Your name will be added to the block list on EVERY social site," I said, standing to my feet.

Harmony looked at me, shaking her head. "Ma, you so lame. I don't need old people following me anyway, so PEAACCCEEE OOOUUUTTTT," she said, mocking Smokey off the movie *Friday* before running out of the room.

I hopped in the shower and threw on a pair of ripped Dolce&Gabbana jeans, a low-cut V-neck shirt and a pair of Jimmy Choo suede boots that came up to my knees. I took the bonnet off my head and let the loose curls fall down my back, then I applied edge control and light makeup, grabbed my Louie bag, and headed out the room. I knocked on Harmony's door lightly before letting myself in, and she was laid across her bed on her Mac laptop.

"OK, I see you wanna get left," I said, placing my hands on my hip.

"Ma, it just took you nine hours to get dressed, now you wanna leave me for taking nine seconds to put on my shoes," she replied, going over to her closet and grabbing a pair of blue and black Mikes to complete her outfit.

"Just come on," I said, turning and walking out of her room as the sound of my alarm system alerted me that someone was coming through the front door.

"I guess nobody on this fake-ass estate rings the doorbell, huh?" I yelled out to an uninvited Courtney.

"Girl, shut up. It ain't like you got a man in here or nothing, dry ass!" Courtney yelled back.

"A'ight, Ma, come on," Harmony said, joining us in the living room.

"Where y'all finna go? I'm going," Courtney stated.

"To the mall, and if you going, then come on," I snapped, walking past them both, heading out the door to my red Range Rover.

"What's her problem?" I heard Courtney whisper to Harmony.

"I have no idea, that's YO' cousin," my daughter replied as they both giggled and closed the front door.

We shopped until we couldn't shop anymore. I promised to bring Harmony to the mall so she could pick up the tennis bracelet she had custom-made a couple weeks ago from the jewelry store. I had no intentions of spending over five thousand dollars. With all that walking and spending, we had built up an appetite, so we headed to get something to eat.

"So, what you finna order?" Courtney asked from across the table at our favorite steakhouse.

"Probably just a salad. You know I'm doing that

whole 'no meat for a month' fast," I explained.

"You better than me, I need all the meat," she replied.

"Since when?" I said, laughing hysterically.

Courtney looked at me and twisted her head to the side.

"Really, Princess? A lesbian joke in front of your ten-year-old daughter, how mature of you," she said, trying not to laugh.

"Girl, shut up. She ain't catch on, did you, Harmony?" I asked, just to make sure.

"Naw, but using context clues, I know now that it has something to do with Courtney dating women, but I learned in school that being gay is perfectly normal, and Courtney, I love you regardless of who you choose to love," Harmony said, taking a sip of her Sprite.

"See," was all I said before we all burst out laughing.

Growing up, who would have ever thought that Miss Bad and Bougie herself would be a lesbian. I should have seen all the signs because when I lost my virginity to Pierre and told her about it, detail for detail, she seemed more disgusted than interested. And then when she was eighteen years old and still a virgin, I questioned that, too. To this day, she claimed that I had scarred her when I got pregnant with Harmony my very first time having sex, but I knew that was some bullshit. Courtney just seemed to like what she liked, and that had nothing to do with me.

"So, Ma, they having a father-daughter dance at my school; you think PaPa will go with me?" she asked, out the blue.

Hearing those words leave my baby's mouth made my heart hurt. I knew the day would come when there would be dances and Father's Day would raise questions, but I wasn't ready yet. Harmony was old enough to understand her father's absence, but was she ready to deal with it?

"Of course, Uncle Quincy would go with you, Harmony. You know your granddaddy will do anything to make you happy," Courtney replied for me, followed by a wink.

I, too, smiled at her. Courtney always came through in the clutch. Without her and my parents, I wouldn't know what to do or how I would have even raised a baby, being that I was a baby myself. I just thanked God that Harmony stopped asking questions about her father. She had finally come to terms with his death, even though she had never met him. Pierre had died in a car crash, three months after I found out I was pregnant. That blow to the head from Stephanie when I was fourteen sent me to the hospital, and that was when I found out I was pregnant with her. My parents took the news hard, and it kind of built a wall between my mother and me, while it actually made my father and I closer. I was always a fan of my father, but after I got pregnant, I really became a daddy's girl.

"Are you coming to the club tonight?" Courtney asked, changing the subject.

"Yeah, the liquor vendors coming in to restock before we open," I replied.

"Aw, yeah, that's right, I forgot. How did the paperwork turn out for Taylor-Made?"

"Everything is cool. All the numbers were accurate, so we good," I said, taking a sip of my lemon water.

"Taylor-Made" was mine and Courtney's construction company, and *"Daddy's Girl"* was the name of the strip club we owned as well. You see, unlike our mothers, we had our money invested in things other than a man. My mother and Aunt Domo, to this day, just lived off our fathers. They were completely content with being rich wives while me, on the other hand, preferred to be a self-made rich bitch. Now, don't get me wrong, I love my mom dearly, and I was not knocking what she did, however, I didn't think it was the smartest thing to do. When dealing with men of my father's caliber, you had to deal with the bullshit that came along with it. There was no way in hell she signed a prenup, and if my father ever decided to just up and leave, he could and take it all from her. I could never see myself going out like that.

After leaving the steakhouse, we headed back to our estate, and I took Harmony directly to my parents' house so Courtney and I could head over to the club. As we were walking in, two of my father's and Uncle Quintin's most loyal workers walked out, and I could tell by the looks on their faces that whatever had just happened behind those doors wasn't good for business.

"Goodnight, ladies," one of them said while the other nodded in our direction.

"Goodnight," the three of us said in unison as we walked into the huge mansion.

"Hey, Ms. Lula, where is my father?" I asked the housekeeper.

"He's downstairs in the basement," she responded in a heavy Spanish accent.

Courtney, Harmony and I headed down the stairs where we found my father and Uncle Quintin sitting on the red leather couch, smoking two huge Cuban cigars. I'd studied my father my entire life, so I could look at the man and know every emotion he felt at that moment, just from his body language. I knew when he was happy, mad, excited; hell, I even knew when he was constipated. Everyone referred to my father as the "evil twin," but to me, he was actually the complete opposite. He was the kindest man on the planet, and the most understanding person I'd ever met. I remember the night I found out I was pregnant with Harmony. After we came home from the hospital, my mother let me have it.

2005

"We give you everything you want, anything you ask for, and how do you repay us? Huh? By giving us a grandchild. Princess, you are only fourteen years old!" my mother screamed at the top of her lungs.

I sat at the kitchen table in tears. I never meant for any of this to happen. How was I supposed to know that losing my virginity and getting pregnant would happen at the same time? It was just supposed to be painful; that's it, that's all.

"I'm sorry, mommy. I'm sorry," I sobbed.

"It's too fucking late to be sorry. I had no idea I was raising a little hoe!" she yelled, slamming her wine glass on the counter, breaking it, causing me to jump.

"Tamika, you better watch your fucking mouth. I know you are upset, but you will not disrespect my child," my father finally spoke.

I looked up briefly and caught my mother darting

her eyes at my father, who didn't seem to be moved by my mother's stares one bit.

"Quincy, I can't believe you are taking up for her at a time like this. How are we going to explain to the rest of the family that our little girl is a fucking slut?"

Before I could blink, my father had my mother leaning backwards over the sink with his hands wrapped around her throat. I noticed the veins popping out of my father's strong arms as he strangled her.

"Look, bitch, if you ever speak about my baby like that again, I'll kill you," he said sternly, releasing the grip he had from around my mother's neck.

I watched tears pour from her eyes as she gasped for air, but I didn't feel sorry for her, not one bit. My mother never held her words back when it came to me. Now, this was her first time being bluntly disrespectful, however, from the way my dad had just handled her, I had a feeling this was definitely her last.

"Princess, go upstairs and shower, we will talk more in the morning. I'm disappointed in you, more so for letting that little girl snake you with a bottle than I am about you being pregnant. I love you. Goodnight," my father said, placing a kiss on my forehead and heading back out the front door.

Present Day

"Look at my three favorite girls in the whole wide world," my Uncle Quintin said, acknowledging us first.

"Hey, Uncle Q; hey, PaPa," Harmony replied, walking over to the couch, giving them both a kiss and a hug before taking a seat in between them.

"What's going on, ladies?" my dad asked, leaning forward, putting out the cigar in the ashtray.

"Nothing much, dropping Harmony off so we can head to the club," I replied.

"Business good?" he asked.

"Never been better," Courtney shot back.

"See, that's the shit I like to hear," my Uncle Q added.

"What shit you like to hear?" I heard my mother's voice from behind us.

"Business, baby. We just talking business," my father said, getting up from the couch.

Harmony got up with him and ran over to my mother, giving her a huge hug.

"Granny baby, what's up, gorgeous?" she said, brushing Harmony's hair with her hand.

"Hey, Glam-Ma. I'm spending the night over here with y'all tonight," Harmony said.

"Oh, is that right? Well, we gotta get us some snacks and catch up on our shows," my mom said, grabbing Harmony by the hand, guiding her upstairs.

Contrary to the way my mother had reacted when she found out I was having Harmony, Harmony was the best thing that had happened to her. My mom loved that little girl's dirty drawers, and so did everyone else in the family.

"A'ight, well, we gotta get going," I said, tapping

Courtney on the arm as she texted away on her phone.

"OK, y'all be safe," Uncle Q said to us as we made our way up the stairs, headed to work.

JA

"Oh my God, Javaris, put the gun down, now!" Skylar screamed at the top of her lungs.

"Maaaaaaaa, tell Javaris to put the gun down. Your ass is crazy!" my little sister yelled in my ear as she hit me on my back.

I held her boyfriend Nick by the collar with one hand as my pistol accompanied the other hand. This was the second time this little motherfucker had been caught in her room. The first time the shit happened, my mom talked me out of beating his ass, but this time, I doubt if he would be so lucky.

My baby sister Skylar was seventeen and in her last year of high school. The deal was, no boys until she walked across the stage, but when she came crying to my OG about six months ago, talking about how she was in love but couldn't really be happy because of me, I agreed to let her date, but fucking was completely out of the question.

They were allowed to do the normal shit like talk on the phone, dates to the movies, I even agreed to let the ugly motherfucker come over, but they were to sit in the living room only, and either my OG or myself had to be present. So, imagine the look on my face when Moms and I pulled up in the driveway at the same time, and Nick's beat-up ass Nissan Maxima was parked a couple houses down.

When we came in, they were on the couch, but I could tell by the way he was sweating, they hadn't been there long. Skylar and my mother thought I was overprotective, but I was seventeen once, and I knew how these little niggas thought. The only thing they cared about was getting their dicks wet, and I'd broken enough hearts growing up, so I had to ensure no nigga ever played my little sister the way I had played bitches. The way Javaris thought at twenty-seven was nowhere on the same playing field as I did at seventeen.

"Man, what the fuck I tell you the last time I caught you in here?" I asked the scared teen.

"Y-y-you said not to let it happen again," he stuttered.

"So, nigga, you take me as a joke, huh?" I asked, really wanting to know the answer.

"Hell naw, JA, but we was just finishing up our senior project," he replied.

"NIGGA, STOP LYING! You must think I'm dumb. You and Skylar don't have not one motherfuckin' class together this year, so how the fuck y'all working on a project together?" I asked, waiting to hear his answer, which was taking too long for him to give me.

"Huh? Huh? This nigga think I'm dumb. Both of y'all must think I'm dumb," I said, waving the pistol back and forth between Skylar and Nick.

"Nick, I told you not to lie to him. Somehow, someway, my brother knows everything. I'm sorry," she said apologizing.

"Javaris, put the gun away and let the boy go home," my mom said, finally stepping in.

"Nah, Ma, he needs to know the consequences of being disrespectful," I said, cocking my pistol.

"JA, NOOOOOOO!!!" Skylar cried out, but once again, I ignored her.

"Nigga, do you know who the fuck I am?" I asked as I watched tears escape the young man's eyes.

"HUH? ANSWER ME!" I yelled, causing him to jump.

"Ye-ye-yeah, Ja, I know who you are, and I apologize. I love your sister, and we just want to be together, that's all," he said as he tried to hold the rest of his tears back.

"Love? Y'all don't know shit about love," I laughed.

"We do, Javaris, that's clearly something you don't know about," my little sister said as she cried in my mother's arms.

I hated to see Skylar hurt, but I hated her being disrespectful even more. I knew that I couldn't protect her forever, but at this moment, I could, and that was what I planned on doing. There was no way possible for me to stop her from dating, and I knew when she went off to school next year, she was going to have all the freedom in the world, and that was when all my protective ways would come back and bite me in the ass.

"I swear to God, JA, I won't come over here ever again," I heard Nick say, snapping me out of my trance.

"When I approached you last time about being here, what did I tell you?" I asked.

"You said you would kill me and not think twice about it," he replied.

"So, you ready to die then, nigga?" I asked with a straight face.

"Nah, but I love your sister, and if that's what it comes down to, then it's whatever," he mustered up enough courage to say.

"A'ight," was all I said before pulling the trigger.

CLICK!

My sister's and mother's screams echoed through the house as I released my grip on Nick, causing his body to fall to the floor.

"I hate you," Skylar said as she punched me in the back while I walked to the front door.

I turned around and watched Nick get up from the ground as he checked his body for blood and bullet holes. I could have easily killed him, but that would have only caused bigger problems, my little sister hating me being the worst of them. There was absolutely nothing I could do to stop her from growing up, I just prayed karma had mercy on her soul because I'd done nothing but dog women out in my days.

"Sky, give your car keys to Ma; you on punishment for the next month. Nick, take yo' black ass home and don't come over here again. I'll be to drop and pick you up from school the rest of this week, and anytime Mom leaves the house, you leave. If not, then I'm coming over here and staying with you," I said, walking out of my mom's six-bedroom house and to my black Range Rover.

I knew Sky hated my guts right now, but this was the way shit was. I was not only her brother but the only father figure she had in her life. Our father was killed in a shootout with the Feds when I was ten, and my mother was pregnant with Sky. Our father was well known, not just in Chicago, but in every state. They nicknamed him Muscle, not only because the nigga was 6'5, and 280 pounds of muscle, but because he was powerful and extremely forceful. He was a known killer then, and his name and legacy still lived on in the streets today. My old man was best friends with Quincy Taylor. Quincy, alongside with his twin brother, ran the biggest and most successful cartel in the Mid-west. The twins were the brains of the operation, and well, Muscle was the muscle.

After my father was killed, the twins made sure my mother was straight. She never had to work a day in her life when my father was alive, and even after he was gone. It was cool living a lifestyle where you had all the Jordans growing up and all the designer shit, but even those things couldn't fill the void of an absent father, so like many young boys, I turned to the streets. I started selling weed in high school, fucked around and got caught, and was sent to an alternative school. My mom was fed up with my ass, so she reached out to the twins for some manly guidance, but instead of leading me in the right direction, they turned me on to some real game. To this day, Quincy talked about how my eyes lit up like a Christmas tree when I spoke about the money and drug game. They said that was the same look my father displayed, and that was how they knew I had it in me.

Starting off, I was just the little big nigga in the streets. I was supplying all the weed at my new school. The twins told me that the only way I'd get my own block was if I actually graduated from high school, so I walked my thirsty ass across the stage two months earlier than planned. After securing the blocks with weed at eighteen, I then went to them and let them know that I needed more, and by more, I meant that white stuff. They took a risk with my young ass but made sure to show me all the ropes, and that was why at twenty-seven years old, I was now the little nigga that the big niggas looked up to. I had the brains of the Taylor Twins and the power of my father. I wasn't to be fucked with. This was something I knew, as well as the streets of Chicago.

PRINCESS

"OK, I need that over there, and those chairs on the side of the stage. Big Al, can you make sure all the rooms in the back is ready?"

My pops' favorite line was, *"Want something done right, you gotta do it yourself,"* and that was exactly why I was setting up for tonight's event. Saturday nights meant a packed house at "Daddy's Girl". Now, there weren't many strip clubs in Chicago, but the few that were here were wack as hell. Either they had old, white bitches with saggy titties or black hoes with bullet holes.

When Courtney turned twenty-one, we went to Miami and visited King of Diamonds. I fell in love with the atmosphere while Courtney fell in love with the bitches. When I say they had some dope-ass chicks sliding down those poles, I meant that shit. Those ladies looked like they had just gotten up from Dr. Miami's or Dr. Curves' operation table. I was fascinated by the shit, went back home, and told my dad and uncle. They said as long as we put our all in it, they'd support us one hundred percent, and that was what they did.

After realizing the Chicago strippers weren't as dope as the Miami and Atlanta ones, we went recruiting. We invaded all the big strip clubs down south, placed an offer on the table that they couldn't refuse, and relocated them. You wouldn't believe the amount of money we were bringing in at the door alone. Our average dancers made close to two thousand a night while the heavy hitters were stuffing close to five thousand in their gym bags. Shit, there were times I wished I was shaking my ass instead of sitting in the office, but I didn't have a lick of rhythm, so I stuck to what I knew.

By midnight, the place was packed from wall to wall, and there was a two-hour wait just to get inside the private rooms. We were getting so much business, we had to add a second dance floor on the second level just to accompany everybody, and that shit drove the customers crazy. Niggas loved the option of seeing two dancers at once, and if it was "Tag-team Thursday," then there were two chicks on each stage.

I had a personal relationship with each and every one of my employees. I made sure that the ladies were straight, happy at work, and happy at home. I didn't want bullshit from their personal life affecting my business because when it came down to my money, I wasn't to be fucked with.

"You in here trying to look all busy and shit."

I looked up from the stack of papers in front of me at Courtney, who walked in wearing a pair of skin-tight black jeans that looked painted on, a belly top that showed off her small waist and six-inch, open toe Giuseppe heels.

"What's up, Princess?" Mocha, Courtney's girlfriend, said, walking in behind her wearing a tight, red dress.

"Hey, y'all, what's up?" I greeted both of them before turning my attention back to the papers in front of me.

"This place is lit tonight. I kind of want to get my ass on the stage and make a couple of stacks myself. Ya know, for old times' sake," Mocha said, laughing a little, but I could tell from the look in her eyes that she was in fact dead ass serious.

My eyes shifted from hers to Courtney, who looked like she was trying to keep it cool.

"For old times' sake my ass. You shouldn't even be thinking about no shit like that," Courtney replied, unable to hold it in any longer.

Courtney and Mocha started dating a little while after I hired Mocha to work for us. She was pretty decent at what she did, but when things started to get serious between the two, Courtney let her know that no woman of hers would be dancing at a strip club. The nerve of her, I know, but Mocha being head over heels in love with my cousin, quit. At first, I was upset with Courtney. Mocha was not the first dancer from our establishment that she'd been intimate with, but I guess there was something about Mocha's chocolate skin and curves that made her really settle down.

"Yeah, I'm thinking about doing some more hiring," I finally spoke, ignoring their argument.

"Yeah, either that or let's open another one," Courtney said, sitting on the edge of my cherry-oak desk.

"Bitch, please. You barely help me with this one, talking *about 'let's open another one'.* You better get the fuck up outta here," I replied, rolling my eyes.

Both Courtney and Mocha laughed. "Why are you so angry? Damn, cousin, you need a hug?"

"Naw, bae, I think she need some dick, or pussy, because I be seeing how all those hoes out there be on her, thinking she a stripper and shit," Mocha added.

"First of all, fuck you and fuck you," I said, sticking my middle finger up and shifting it in the air between the two. "And, second of all, I don't need no man to make me happy. And last, but damn sure not least, I leave all the carpet munching to you two. I'm definitely good on that," I continued.

I loved my cousin, and even loved me some Mocha, but these two bitches were starting to aggravate me. They always used the fact that since I hadn't been with a man for real in my adult life that something was wrong with me, but I was perfectly fine. Yeah, I got lonely and got tired of playing with myself, but the fact that I'd been celibate for the past five years really meant something to me.

"A'ight, Erica and Cyn, if y'all don't mind, I'd like to get back to work. Thanks for stopping by."

I always called them Erica and Cyn from the reality show *Love & Hip Hop* because they looked more like best friends than lovers. They were both girly girls, and although Courtney was the aggressor, she was still a soft-ass bitch.

They both stood, flipped their long weaves, and walked out, which only proved my point even more. Once the door was closed, I got back to work, but something told me to look at the monitor that was mounted on the wall. The TV provided me with every angle of the club, and it was the view at the bar that drew my attention. There were three men dressed in all black, standing there, looking around. Neither of them had a cup in their hands, and they paid none of the beautiful women who surrounded them any mind. They stood there with mugs on their faces, and that was how I knew they didn't belong.

I shot Nino, one of my father's workers who vacationed at the club frequently, a text to let him know what was going on before I made my way down to the main level.

"Hello, gentleman, having a good time? Can I get you guys anything? Maybe a drink, a dance or something?" I asked once I approached the three men.

All three of them looked at me but didn't utter a word. My number one pet peeve was being ignored, so I tried again. Maybe it was the loud music, maybe they didn't hear me.

"Can I help you fellas with anything?" I asked, this time much louder.

"Look, bitch, you can get the fuck out of our face, that's what the fuck you can do," the taller one said, never looking at me.

My face instantly screwed up. I hated a disrespectful-ass nigga, and the way I was raised, disrespect was something that should never be taken lightly.

"Aye, look, the bitch still standing here. BYE!" he yelled, causing Larry and Curly to laugh.

"I'm going to have to ask y'all to leave," I said, trying my best not to act up.

"We ain't going no-muthafucking-where," the shorter one spoke.

OK, Princess, count to ten. One…two…three… This had been a routine since I was younger. Sometimes it worked, sometimes it didn't, and this was one of the times it didn't.

Before I knew it, I reached behind my back and pulled my pistol from under my shirt, pointing it to the beer belly of the dude closest to me discreetly

"Look, li'l bitch, I don't want to act a fool in this here nice place, but I swear to God if I have to ask you and your homies to leave again, y'all leaving out this motherfucker in body bags," I said through clenched teeth.

The guy looked at me in the eyes with a blank expression, and then down at the gun that was poking him before looking back at me, this time with a twisted grin. I could tell he was about to act a fool, but the sounds of more guns being cocked in his ears muted him. They were surrounded by Nino and about five more of my father's people with drawn guns. That once tough demeanor quickly faded, and the bitch in him came out. Seconds later, in an orderly fashion, they made their exit.

"Your ass need help," Courtney said, storming into my office yet again, this time by herself.

"What?" I asked, clueless.

"Your anger. What if you pulling that gun out on those niggaz would have turned into something else, something bigger, something unnecessary, something deadly?" she lectured me.

"OK, but it didn't. The fuck you tripping for?" I shot back.

"I'm tripping because ever since we were kids, you had an issue with your anger."

"NO! I have an issue with disrespect, those are two different things," I said in my defense. "And besides, everything went smooth, the crowd didn't even notice," I continued.

Courtney just stood there with her hands on her hips, shaking her head.

"For real, yo, you need help. And I'm calling Uncle Q and telling on you," she said, grabbing her phone and walking out of my office for good.

JA

"I can't believe you really over here. Don't you supposed to be selling some drugs or something?" Sky said as I sat across from her at the kitchen table while she did her homework.

"Number one, watch yo' mouth. Number two, these hands don't touch no fucking drugs. Number three, you must have thought I was playing when I said, if Mama not here, then I will be," I replied, getting up from the table, going over to the refrigerator.

Sky let out a loud sigh, indicating that she was frustrated, but I didn't care; she had to learn the hard way.

"JA, you treat me like I'm a baby and I hate that. I said I was sorry and that it'll never happen again, why can't you just trust me?" she whined.

"I can't trust you because you've proven already that you can't be trusted. Plain and simple, now focus on that homework," I responded, walking off to answer the doorbell.

"What's up, my nigga?" I said to Smoke as I opened the front door to my mother's house.

"What's up, nigga? What's going on, Sky?" he said, going straight to the cabinets and grabbing a bag of chips.

"Tuh," Sky said, rolling her eyes, ignoring Smoke.

"What the fuck is wrong with her?" Smoke asked.

"Shit, it ain't nothing she won't get over. What's going on with you?" I asked my best friend.

"Mannnnn, look, I just almost caught a domestic

fucking with Kayla's crazy ass. That bitch gon' come up missing. I swear to God on my momma," Smoke grunted.

Kayla was Smoke's baby momma, and that bitch gave my mans a hard time about everything. Him and her being into it was nothing new, so I didn't even bother prying, trying to get more information. If you'd heard one story, then you'd heard them all.

"Y'all asses crazy. You talked to Mack Maine about that shipment?" I asked, changing the subject.

"Aw, yeah, everything straight. I just hung up with him before I came in here," he assured me.

"Cool. Cool. Cool," I said rubbing my hands through my full beard and laying back on the couch.

"I'm done, daddy, can I please be excused?" Sky yelled from the kitchen.

I shook my head before getting up and going in there to join her.

"Let me see," I said, reaching for her paper.

"See what?" she asked, screwing up her face.

"Yo' homework, motherfucker. Let me check it."

"Javaris, are you serious right now?"

"I'm dead ass, bruh, now hand it here," I replied, snatching the papers out her hands.

I scanned over the math problems before handing it back to her.

"Excellent job, but number five is wrong," I told her.

"What you mean, it's wrong? I know it's right," she fussed, looking over her calculations.

"Skylar, the force of gravity is 49 N, which means each of the two cables must pull upwards with 24.5 N of force. I mean, you got the concept, you were just off by one number." I laughed before walking away.

"I HATE YOOUUUU!" she yelled.

"The nigga been a pretty nerd all his life," Smoke said as I walked past him, going back into the living room.

I grabbed my phone off the table and noticed I had seven missed calls and five text messages. I went to the messages first, and they were all from Tika.

Tika: Wyd?

Tika: WYA?

Tika: JA why must you ignore me?

Tika: Answer your phone.

Tika: I FUCKING HATE YOU!!!!

I deleted all the messages and put my phone down, then I grabbed the remote and turned to ESPN. I was always handling business, so I never had time to just chill and watch TV. While Smoke fried some chicken in the kitchen, I caught up on some highlights from last night's game.

"Aye, Lebron gon' fuck them boys up again this year," Smoke said, walking into the front with a plate of hot wings and an Orange Fanta pop.

"Aye, my dude, you sound crazy. Curry ain't going,

you see them boys' record? You got us fucked up!" I argued.

"Nigga, you only saying that because you light skin. The whole team full of light skin niggaz. You swear y'all making a comeback."

"Comeback? Nigga, we ain't never went nowhere. You just witnessed how my homie Drake bodied Meek. Y'all better stop sleeping on the light skins."

Just as Smoke was about to get hyped, ready to be the spokesperson for all dark-skinned niggas, the front door opened and my OG walked in carrying shopping bags.

"What's up, Ma?"

"What's up, Ma?" Smoke said behind me.

"Hey, boys. Smoke, I know damn well you not eating in my living room. Have you lost your fucking mind?" she said, dropping her bags and walking over to where we were.

"Nah, Ma, I was eating in the kitchen, and JA asked me for some, so I said, 'Nah, nigga, you better come in this kitchen with me if you want some, you know Ma don't play that eating in her front shit.' So this nigga says, 'She ain't here, nigga, and I pay the mortgage on this motherfucker, so I can eat where I want.' I was like, 'Hell naw, I respect the rules in Ms. Carter's house, but you know he light skin and feels like he can do whatever he wants.'," Smoke rambled.

My mother and I burst out laughing. I see why he was always into it with his baby momma because all he did was lie.

"A'ight, Ma, I'm up outta here. Sky finished her

homework. I'll let you know if I'll be able to drop her off tonight or not. Calvin having a grand opening tonight at his club, so if I ain't somewhere slumped over, I'll be here."

"OK, baby, be safe," she said, kissing my cheek.

"Fa'sho," I replied, walking out with Smoke in tow.

PRINCESS

"Could you pleeaasseee speed this bitch up? I gotta pee, Courtney," I whined, squeezing my legs together as we exited the expressway.

"Damn, Princess, I'm going as fast I can without getting pulled over. You worse than Harmony. I'ma have to make sure your grown ass uses it before we leave the house."

I wasn't trying to hear shit Courtney had to say, I just needed to make it to Mocha's condo before I pissed in her $100,000 car. Courtney must have read my mind because before I knew it, we pulled into the parking garage.

"Why the fuck you ain't call her so she could have the door opened already?" I asked as I watched my cousin fidget with her keys.

Courtney paused all movement and looked at me, letting me know I was working her last nerves. I placed my fingers up to my lips, motioning that I was zipping my mouth closed and throwing away the key. I figured she'd move faster without me nagging in her ear, but I really, really had to pee.

"Thank God!" I said to myself as the door opened.

I pushed Courtney out the way and ran to the back of the house where the bathroom was located. I didn't even bother speaking to Mocha or to the two men who were chilling in her living room. I had to piss first; I'd apologize for my rude behavior later. After I relieved myself, I washed my hands and stared at my reflection in the mirror. I wasn't sure how I had allowed Courtney and Mocha to talk me into going to some club tonight. I had plans to go in the crib and chill with my baby girl on this Thursday night.

Who in the fuck had a grand opening on a Thursday, anyway? Nonetheless, when Courtney ran a script on me about this club possibly being "Daddy's Girl's" competition, I figured she made sense, and it wouldn't hurt to see what was to it.

I fixed my bone straight weave, applied another coat of MAC lip gloss and exited the bathroom.

"Hellloooo," I sang as I entered the room.

"Sup, Princess? Princess, this is my cousin, Smoke, and his homie, JA. JA and Smoke, this is Courtney's cousin, Princess," Mocha said, introducing us all.

"What's up!" both of them said at the same time.

"Damn, she fine. Damn, you fine. Mocha, is she gay, too?" Smoke asked, looking me up and down, causing us all to laugh.

"Nah, cuzn, she's not gay," Mocha answered between giggles.

"Good because I ain't either. Hey, I'm Smoke, how you doing?" he said, sliding over to where I was standing.

"I'm good," I replied, still trying to control my laughter.

Smoke was an "OK" looking dude. He put me in the mind of the rapper, Fabolous. He was tall and skinny, but I think it was the chipped tooth that really did it for me.

"So, y'all coming out with us tonight?" Smoke asked, putting his arm around my shoulders.

"Yeah, we are stopping by for a few minutes. Clubs ain't really my thing," I said, looking at him out the side of my eye.

"This fucking girl is crazy. The only person I know that hollers she don't like clubs but owns a strip club," Courtney said from the kitchen.

"Aw, word, you own a strip club? Which one?" Smoke inquired.

"Daddy's Girl, it's out South on 187th," I replied.

"Aye, I heard that bitch be cracking. Me and JA gotta swing through one night and holler at you, ain't that right, JA?"

"Nigga, you know I don't fuck with no strippers, but you have fun," his quiet homie responded.

"What the fuck wrong with strippers, JA?" Mocha asked, clearly offended as she stood with her hands on her hips.

"Aw, nah, baby, no offense to you. You know it ain't even like that. I'm just not a fan," Ja replied.

"Yeah, me either, but I ain't here to judge. Besides, it's a lucrative business, and all my girls' bank accounts hold five digits or more so…," I said, shrugging.

"A boss. Yeah, I think we gon' be a power couple," Smoke said, walking back over to the couch, joining JA.

"A'ight, y'all, let's go!" Mocha yelled as she came from the back with her purse in hand.

Both men stood up from the couch, and it wasn't until then that I noticed how fine JA really was. The first thing that caught my eye was his height; he had to be at least 6'4. He definitely looked like he belonged in the

NBA. He wasn't a heavy dude, but he was nowhere as skinny as Smoke was. I would for sure say he had an average build. And then there were those tattoos all over his neck and arms. At first glance, I wasn't sure, but now that I was standing so close, I was pretty sure he had to be mixed with something of Spanish descent. His light complexion and fine hair gave it away. He had the perfect mixture of a pretty nigga but hood nigga swag, if that made any sense. Sure, I encountered handsome men on a daily basis, but this man right here was the truth.

We all walked to the door and out to the hallway as Courtney held the elevator for us.

"Ladies first," JA said, motioning with his hands for me to go ahead of him.

"Awwww, him might not like strippers, but he's a gentleman," I teased.

He looked at me and smiled, slightly biting his bottom lip. "Yeah, when I wanna be, now get yo' ass on this elevator."

Mocha joined us in Courtney's car as the men went in the opposite direction. The whole ride, I couldn't get this nigga's facc out of my head, he was just that fine. I wasn't sure if I was a fan of his personality, but when it came to his looks, I was a groupie.

"So, your cousin Smoke drove, or his homie?" I asked out of the blue.

"They took JA's car. Why?" Mocha answered.

"I was just asking," I responded, looking back out the window.

"Just ask what type of car the nigga drive, Princess,

and stop beating around the bush," Courtney blurted.

"Girl, what the fuck is you talking about?" I asked, rolling my eyes.

"Every time Princess is remotely interested in a nigga, she tries to figure out what type of nigga he is by the type of car he drives," she answered.

Mocha looked back at me and started laughing.

"Shut up, bitch, that is not true. You make me seem all shallow and shit."

"Well, cousin, it is what it is," Courtney stated.

"Baby, leave the princess alone. But to answer your question, I believe JA is in his Maserati tonight, or maybe the Porsche Shit, I don't know, but he got a Benz truck, too," Mocha said.

"And just like that, my back seats are wet," Courtney alleged, followed by them laughing.

"Girl, you is showing out tonight," I said, rolling my eyes from the back seat.

I was getting annoyed by Courtney and her ability to read me like an open book. I hated that that bitch had been around me all my life and knew me better than I knew myself sometimes.

"Nah, bitch, you showing out tonight, but I'm happy. A bit confused, but happy, nonetheless," Courtney said.

"But what's to be confused about?" I pondered.

"You ain't had no dick since King died, yet you

base the niggaz that you are the least bit interested in off their cars. You weird as fuck, bruh," she explained.

"How? How Sway? You can tell a lot about a man by the car he drives," I snapped.

"That's that shallow shit again. A nigga can be rich, driving a Charger because that's simply what he likes and a nigga can have a Beamer that he's hiding at his mommy house because he's behind on payments and they're about to take that motherfucker," she explained.

"You know what, this might be the first time you right," I agreed.

"Nah, Courtney, you dead ass wrong about this one, though. JA got stupid money. I can't tell you exactly what the man do, but whatever it is, he do it big. Him and my cousin Smoke been friends since they were little. Smoke lived with us after my auntie died, and I've watched him and JA both grow up. Neither one of them are your average hustlers; they got that Pablo work, if you know what I mean," Mocha explained. "Oh, and the nigga own a sports bar and two laundromats," she added.

He had to be cleaning his money. My father hadn't exposed me to his business firsthand. Hell, I'd only seen like four of the men who worked for them ever in my life and I knew there were a lot more. My pops and uncle had a few businesses of their own, so I knew exactly what type of work this man did. It was kind of intriguing and turning me on, but when you hadn't had dick in years, the way the wind blew turned me on sometimes.

The club was packed, and the place was nice as fuck. They had two levels like my place, but they had a bar on both levels, something I had actually thought about stealing. The DJ booth was high above us in the middle of the floor, and he had been killing shit since we'd walked through the door. The section we were in was huge. There was a large, cream sectional couch, and the table in front had bottles of every liquor you could think of on it. I couldn't front, I was actually enjoying the vibe.

"Look," Courtney whispered to me, followed by an elbow nudge.

I followed her eyes and watched JA walk towards us. He wore all black, and the only color came from the white diamonds that danced on his ears, neck, fingers and chain. I never understood why niggas wore shades in the club, but this man was wearing the fuck out of these Eazy E Locs.

"Damn, where y'all go after y'all left my crib?" Mocha yelled over the music.

"We had to handle some business," Smoke said, sitting on the left side of me.

I watched JA talk to a few people around him before finally joining us.

"Aye, scoot over," he said, towering over me as I did what I was told.

Two cups, toast up with the gang
From food stamps, to a whole nother domain
Out the bottom, I'm a living proof
They compromising, half a million on the coupe
Drug houses, looking like Peru
Graduated, I was overdue
Pink molly, I can barely move
Ask about me, I'm going bust a move
Rick James, 33 chains
Old Chanel, cruising Biscayne

Top off, that's a liability
Hit the gas, boosting my adrenaline

Future had a way with street niggas because this man barely bobbed his head to the other music, but when this shit came on, he stood up and everything. You would have thought he was in the video. I couldn't help but stand there and admire the way he moved. Future must have had the same effect on women because, by the second verse, I was standing next to him, rapping along.

Before the Maybach, I'd drive anything
Buy my Range, make 'em go insane
My guillotine, drank promethazine

He glanced over at me and smirked, showing off one dimple that I hadn't noticed before. I winked at him and kept rapping along. I made a mental note to buy Courtney lunch tomorrow because if it weren't for that bitch, I wouldn't be here, having the most fun I'd had in a while.

JA

First thing I noticed when she ran into Mocha's crib was her ass. I guess that was because it was the only thing I actually got a chance to see, but when she walked out the bathroom, smiling, I swear to God, it seemed to light up the whole house. I knew the shit might sound corny coming from a nigga like me, but this was the only way I could explain it. Ms. Boss Lady looked to be about 5'7 with the shape bitches paid top dollar for. Not to say her shit wasn't paid for, but either way it went, I wasn't knocking it. Her hair was long, a funny looking brown that matched her eyes, and she wore it draped down her back. She was wearing an all-black dress that looked painted on, and she had to keep pulling it down with her hands because her wide hips made it rise. Her complexion was light brown, and she had a scar on the side of her face like shorty had in the movie *Love & Basketball*. This girl was beyond beautiful, and she looked so familiar, but I knew for a fact that I'd never seen her before because I for sure would've remembered.

After Future's hit "Mask Off" went off, the DJ kept the tempo going by playing Migos. Now, at the age of twenty-seven, I was considered an older nigga, but I couldn't front, this new generation's music, wasn't talking about shit lyrically, but it got a motherfucker hype. Princess stepped forward a little and rapped along as I stood back and admired the way she moved. The way her ass bounced up and down in her dress had a nigga's dick hard as Chinese Algebra. I wasn't sure if the attraction was based solely off looks, the fact that I knew just from talking to her for five minutes that she was about her business, or the fact that she seemed like one of the homies. It may have been a combination of all three, but this girl had a nigga's mind racing. I had to get her.

"This yo' shit, huh?" I said, walking up and standing behind her, pressing my dick against her ass.

She stopped dancing briefly and turned around. "Can't you tell? Now back up before I give yo' ass the business," she replied, bending over slightly and twerking.

"Do yo' thang, don't let me stop you," I said, holding both of my hands in the air.

Shit, the damage was already done. My dick was already hard, and she was a grown woman. This wasn't her first time, she knew what it was. Now her rhythm was a little off, but baby girl got points for effort, and with an ass like hers, she could literally just stand there; I was sure it could move on its own. Just as she was getting better at it, I felt someone rush me from the back, bumping me, causing Princess to drop her phone and stumble over her heels.

I turned around, ready to shoot any motherfucker in there. I reached for the pistol that was secured in my waistband but calmed down a little when no one was behind me but Tika.

"So, this why the fuck you can't return any of my calls or text messages? You too busy entertaining bitches in the club!" she yelled at the top of her lungs.

I shook my head at her before turning around, making sure Princess was straight. She was picking her phone up off the floor, and whatever text message she was reading caused her to pause.

"I gotta go!" she said, finally looking up at me.

"Why? Is everything OK?" I asked, leaning forward in her ear.

"It's my daughter. I gotta go," she said, preparing to

walk off, but when she tried, Tika stepped in front of her.

"Aw, so this little bum bitch is the one that got you tripping," Tika said, pointing her fingers in Princess' face.

"Tika, you need to chill," I said, pushing her back a few steps away from Princess.

"It's cool, JA," she said, looking at me before stepping closer to Tika's face.

"IF I EVER SEE YOU AGAIN, I'M GOING TO BEAT YO' ASS AND THAT, MY DEAR, IS NOT A THREAT, IT'S A PROMISE," Princess said, smiling before walking over to her cousin, whispering something in her ear before both of them rushed out.

I wanted to stop her, but I could tell she was dealing with something concerning her child and now was not the time. I hoped everything was cool, though, but now I had to deal with this fucked up ass bitch standing in front of me.

"JA, I'm so sick of this shit. Why the fuck can't you just act right?" Tika asked as the tears flowed down her face.

I didn't bother to answer the question. Instead, I walked around her and looked for Smoke. It was time for me to go, and if this nigga wanted a ride, he needed to be ready to bounce, too.

"Aye, Calvin, you seen that nigga Smoke?" I asked my homie, who was also the club owner.

"Yeah, there he go over there," Calvin replied, pointing to the bar where Smoke was talking to some chick.

I made my way over to where he was and waited for the perfect time to interrupt.

"Aye, nigga, I'm about to slide. You riding with me or you good?" I asked.

"I'm right behind you," was all he said before handing the chick he was talking to back her phone.

We went outside the overly packed club and waited for the valet to bring my Porsche around front.

"Ain't that Mocha down there?" I said to Smoke, pointing towards the corner.

"Yeah, let me make sure she's good," he said as we both walked off in her direction.

Mocha was wrapping up a phone call and finishing a blunt when we approached her.

"You good?" Smoke inquired.

"Yeah, I'm about to call an Uber, though, what's up?"

"An Uber for what? Didn't you ride with your girlfriend?" Smoke asked her.

"Aw, yeah, but something happened to Princess' daughter, and they had to leave. I told them to go ahead; I wasn't ready to go yet."

"Will her daughter be straight?" I asked.

"Yeah, she had an allergic reaction to something. They're meeting Princess' parents at the hospital now."

It was good to know that it wasn't anything major going on with shorty and her kid.

"Aw, OK, good, but I'll drop you off. You ain't gotta take no Uber," I said to Mocha.

"You sure there will be enough room?" she replied, confusing me with her response.

"Yeah, why you ask that?" I inquired.

"'Cause here come yo' little girlfriend."

Before I could turn around to see what she was talking about, Tika walked towards us, screaming my name.

"This bitch," I whispered to myself as I held my head low.

"JA, I'm going home with you!" she yelled, walking up.

"Nah, shorty, you going home, but it ain't with me," I said, walking off.

Tika stood there looking shocked, and I had no idea why. This had become a routine with us, and for some reason, the crazy bitch never let go or gave up. I had met Tika about a year ago, and she tricked a nigga. She was cool and down to Earth, and whenever we linked, it was nothing but a good time. Now, from the beginning, we were just fucking. I slid her money to pay her bills and get whatever she wanted simply because I fucked with her like that. About six months ago, I got her pregnant, and I couldn't lie, I was a little excited about it at first, but when I let her know that a baby wouldn't mean her and I were a couple, she couldn't take it and went and got an abortion behind my back. I guess she called herself hurting me, but she ended up being the one hurt. I cut off all ties with her unless I wanted my dick sucked or some convenient pussy, and that was where I fucked up. I swore to myself I was done with this bitch though because she was causing unnecessary problems.

"Aye, man, why y'all don't get y'all homie?" Smoke said to the three girls who were with Tika.

"Yeah, 'cause the bitch out here looking bad," Mocha chimed in.

"Mocha, ain't nobody talking to you," Tika said.

"But ain't nobody gon' do shit about me talking, though," Mocha snapped, flicking her blunt.

"Yeah, friend, let's just go," one of her friends said, pulling her by the arm.

"I swear to God, I hate you!" she screamed before she was completely snatched away.

The three of us stood around a little longer and laughed before Mocha's phone started ringing.

"Hold up, y'all, this Courtney FaceTiming me," she said before answering the phone.

I stood there listening to Courtney give an update on Princess' daughter's condition as well as a little small talk they had about some other shit.

"A'ight, I'm ready," she said, ending the call.

The three of us got into my car and made our way to drop Mocha off.

"Aye, JA, did you get shorty number?" Smoke asked out of the blue.

"What shorty?"

"Princess, JA… did you get Princess' number?" Mocha answered for him.

"Aw, naw, Tika walked up and started talking crazy before I could."

"Damn, for real? That bitch probably scared her off," Smoke said.

"SCARED WHO OFF?" Mocha asked, raising her voice, damn near yelling.

"The Princess chick," Smoke informed her.

"Man, trust and believe, Tika ain't scare Princess' crazy ass off. I'm surprised Princess ain't handle the bitch right then and there, especially if she said something to her directly. When I tell you that bitch is about that life, I mean it. She don't give nooooo fuccckkkk," Mocha added.

For some weird reason, the shit Mocha was telling me turned me on. I had to see shorty again. It was like she had come into my life for a moment, fucked shit up, and dipped out on me. Only thing was, she didn't leave a glass slipper. I had to find her, and that was exactly what I planned on doing.

PRINCESS

"Harmony, I do not care. Your ass not gon' be satisfied until you get hospitalized for real, or even worse, yo' ass end up dead!" I yelled as I backed out of the parking spot in the hospital parking lot.

"Mommy, why are you hollering at me like this?" my baby asked from the passenger side.

"Because you too old for this shit and you know better, Harmony."

"It was only a small piece, though, and I got it from my friend, Melanie," she said in her defense.

"I don't care who you got it from or how big or small it was, you are allergic to peanuts, child."

"But, mommy, it's so good. Like, why I couldn't be allergic to something like chitterlings because that stuff stank and it's nasty."

I tried not to laugh, but I couldn't hold it in. I had no idea what I was going to do with this child of mine. This girl and her love for peanuts was insane, but she had to realize that she just couldn't have them.

"Ayyeeeee, jack! Look, Ma, this our song!" Harmony shouted before turning the volume up on the radio and rapping along.

Percocets, molly, Percocets
Percocets, molly, Percocets
Rep the set, gotta rep the set
Chase a check, never chase a bitch
Mask on, fuck it, mask off
Mask on, fuck it, mask off
Percocets, molly, Percocets

Chase a check, never chase a bitch
Don't chase no bitches

I glanced over at her as she bounced up and down in her seat, dabbing occasionally. I shook my head, focusing my attention back on the road where I unknowingly began to smile. My mind switched back to the club where I envisioned JA and I dancing and rapping along to this same song.

That man, Lord, that man! I couldn't figure out for the life of me where I seemed to have seen him before, but it hit me. He looked exactly like Ryan Henry from VH1's show *Black Ink Chicago*. The light complexion, nicely trimmed beard, fine hair and those tattoos. Now that I thought about it, his ass looked better than Ryan Henry. Outside of his looks, the way he carried himself was attractive. That brief encounter at the club let me know that he was somebody. It was the way the men in there showed him nothing but respect, and when he walked in, bitches were all over him, but that was to be expected. There was something about him, and I had to figure this shit out.

"Mommy, I'm so sleepy," Harmony announced, snapping me out of my wet dream.

I glanced at the clock on the dashboard of my Range Rover and the time read 2:37 a.m. I had left the club a little after midnight, and after sitting in the hospital with this hard-headed ass girl for damn near two hours, I was sleepy myself. I had one of my father's workers bring my truck up to the hospital, so Courtney and Mocha didn't have to sit around and wait for me.

"I'm tired, too, baby, but you really gon' be tired in a few hours when it's time to wake up and go to school," I replied as security opened the gates to the estate for us.

"School? Ma, it's almost three in the morning, and I have to wake up at seven. I'll only have three hours of sleep," she whined.

"You'll have four hours, and that's exactly why you taking yo' non-counting ass to school. I'm getting you a math tutor, by the way," I laughed.

Harmony frowned her face up, but it didn't faze me one bit.

"Ma, I almost died just a few hours ago," she said.

"Well, at least that little piece of Snickers was worth it, now go upstairs and go to sleep."

Harmony stomped up the stairs. She was lucky I was too tired to whoop her ass, but I definitely made a mental note to address that shit in the morning. She was a privileged child, and she knew it. Harmony went to the best school in the area; her classmates were children of politicians, surgeons and judges. Her tuition cost more than an upper-class family's mortgage. I didn't know many kids whose wardrobe consisted of Louie, Gucci and Prada. Now, don't get me wrong, I was not one of those moms. I could find Harmony some shit I liked in Target, and I'd get her that with no problem. I liked what I liked, whether it was $30 or $3,000.

I slipped out of my clothes, leaving them in the middle of my bedroom floor before heading to the connecting bathroom. I turned the water on in the shower, testing it with my hands, getting it as hot as I could stand. I grabbed a towel out of the linen closet and got in. The steam took over the bathroom as the water made love to my body. I grabbed the Dove body wash, lathered my towel and washed up twice. I was sleepy as hell before I got in, and this shower had only made matters worse.

Once I got out, I dried off with my oversized Ralph Lauren Polo towel and exited the hot-ass bathroom. I grabbed a big T-shirt out the drawer, threw it on, and jumped inside my California King bed. I set the alarm on my phone before placing it on the charger, and before I knew it, I was knocked out cold.

The bright sun beamed through the blinds, waking me up seven minutes before my alarm was set to go off. The pettiness in me wanted to stay in bed and get all of my rest, but I knew if I had, I wasn't waking back up anytime soon. I flipped my covers back and slipped on my Chanel house shoes that were nearby and made my way down the hall to Harmony's room.

Her door was cracked open, but it was quiet, so I knew she was still asleep. I peeked my head in and watched her sleep peacefully. The pink flower comforter set partially covered her body, and her long, curly, sandy brown hair rested wildly on her head. I smiled as a warm feeling came across my body. Harmony Pierre Taylor was my lifeline; nothing and no one in this world mattered more than her. Shit was crazy to me because even ten years later, I still couldn't believe I was a mother. She was no doubt the apple of my eye, and I thanked God every second of the day for this blessing.

"WAKE YO' ASS UP, LUCKY CHARMS!!" I yelled, kicking over the chair that was next to her door purposely.

Harmony jumped up quickly, grabbing her heart as if it were about to jump out of her chest and run. The look on her face caused me to bend over and laugh uncontrollably.

"Maaaaaaaa. Why must you play so much? Why

you doooo that?" she cried.

"If you stay ready, you'll never have to get ready," I replied, picking up a few things around her room and placing them in the right spot.

"But you almost made me have a heart attack," she shot back.

"You'll be all right, now get up and shower so we can go."

Just like I thought, Harmony was going to slow poke around and take her time, so that was exactly why I had woken her up thirty minutes before I usually did. After we both got dressed, we headed out the door.

"Ma, it's so hot out here. Why can't I be on summer vacation like regular students?"

"Look, girl, I'm tired of having this conversation with you. Your school is all year round. There are times when you are out on break, and they are in, and vice versa."

I felt like I'd said that same line a hundred million times. She was beginning to work my nerves this morning, so I had to get her ass to school ASAP.

"Huuhhhh, I guess," she replied out of frustration, but I was the one who was frustrated.

We stopped at Starbucks to grab a coffee for me, and a frappe and breakfast sandwich for Harmony. After I got rid of her, I made my way to mine and Courtney's construction company, "Taylor Made". About two years ago, my father and uncle came to us with the idea of starting this company. Everything sounded good, so we took their ideas and ran with it. Surprisingly, Taylor Made had made us richer than Daddy's Girl. It also was less stressful running it. The bulk of our work consisted of a real-estate development team and our sponsor builders. We had the best of the best on our teams. The best architects to manage the jobs, along with the best construction managers, design engineers and project managers. The best part about it all was the feeling of success. Walking or driving past a building, knowing you and your team were responsible for the infrastructure.

"About fucking time," Courtney said, followed by a round of applause when I stepped inside her office.

"Girl, stop. Let's get this meeting started so I can get out of here, I got shit to do," I replied, taking a seat across from her.

Courtney stuck up her middle finger before sliding a stack of manila folders to me.

"OK, these requests just came in. Look them over and tell me what you think… And, ohhhh, bitch, I almost forgot. I didn't get a chance to talk to you last night because of Harmony and her situation, but ummm, what happened? What was going on with you and that fine-ass nigga last night?"

"Girl, who?" I asked, playing dumb.

"Bitch, 'WHO', that owl on your shoulder. You know I'm referring to that nigga JA."

"Aw, him? He a'ight," I lied and replied nonchalantly.

"Just a'ight? That man makes me wanna suck his dick and you know I'm a vegetarian."

My eyes got big, and I couldn't help but laugh because JA could turn Young M.A straight.

"Bitch, you stupid. Tell me why I had a dream about him last night, though," I confessed.

"SWEAR TO GOD!" Courtney screamed, banging her hands on the table.

"Yeah, man, and he fucked the shit out of me," I replied, burying my face in my hands.

"You li'l nasty hoe. I need details, though."

"No, ma'am. No, I'm not finna do this with you. I told you I had to go. Now, back to work. How you want to handle this workload?" I asked, changing the subject.

Courtney rolled her eyes and smacked her lips before looking back at the folders.

"You a lame, bruh, but anyway, I'm going to look over some resumes this weekend and give those who qualify a call on Monday," Courtney continued.

"OK, that's cool. I'm free all day next Thursday, so let's set up the interviews for then. Can you reach out to Mark for me, please, and let him know that I need him on site tomorrow bright and early at seven a.m.," I said before standing, grabbing my Gucci purse off the marble desk.

"A'ight, cool, but where you in a rush to anyway?" she inquired.

"I got a hair appointment," I responded, throwing up the deuces and walking out.

"A HAIR APPOINTMENT? BITCH, THAT AINT NO EMERGENCY!" I heard her yell from the office, but I was already on the elevator.

JA

Blonde and red weave covered my lap as I sat in a chair alongside the bed. Gina and her homegirl, Shana, hit my line after I left the club, trying to link. At first, I wasn't on that, but when she told me she was bringing her buddy along, I figured a two for one wouldn't be so bad, so I had them meet me at the Marriot hotel in Oakbrook. Tika was the only bitch I had ever allowed to come to my house, and we see how that turned out, so whenever I got some free time to entertain bitches, they only got a hotel room; nothing more and nothing less. I wasn't spending the night here with them, and when I bounced, they had to, too. Sometimes I was a gentleman and let them sleep until the morning, but that was based on the type of work they put in on my dick.

"Got damn!" I said, looking down at my lap as Gina sucked my balls and Shana deep throated all ten inches. I could feel my nut building, and although I didn't want this feeling to be over, I had business to take care of in a few hours, so I tilted my head back and released my kids in Shana's mouth. Gina brought her head up and caught whatever Shana let escape. That shit alone almost made me nut again.

After they sucked me dry, Gina got off her knees and went into the bathroom, coming out with a wet towel. She threw it at Shana, who caught it and started wiping off my semi-hard dick. While she was doing so, Gina lifted Shana's body in the air a little and started eating her pussy from the back. From the way Shana was moaning and going crazy, it was evident that Gina had a bomb on the head. She must eat pussy just as good as she sucked dick.

I got up and stepped around the ladies before securing my dick back in my jeans.

"Why you are leaving us, Daddy?" Shana moaned softly.

Instead of responding, I grabbed my keys and pistol off the stand by the door and made my exit.

Once I got inside my Porsche, I placed my phone on the charger and kept my pistol on my lap. I immediately noticed a red Avenger's lights pop on when I pulled away. I stopped at the light on Roosevelt Road, and so did the Avenger. After the light changed, I made a sharp right down a low-key side street, thinking that maybe I was tweaking and the car wasn't actually following me, but my suspicions were confirmed when the Avenger hit that same right, falling for the bait. I quickly grabbed my phone out of the cup holder and placed a call.

"I'm about to slide through, light it up," was all I said to the caller on the other end before hopping on the 290 expressway, heading West.

I made sure to keep a normal speed; I wanted to ensure that whoever was in the Avenger didn't know that I had noticed them. I made my exit at Independence, going East towards Douglas. When I hit the block, I stopped at the stop sign for about twenty seconds before taking off full speed.

POW. POW. POW. POW. POW.

About six shots rang out in the air, and I slowed my car down and looked through the rearview mirror where I noticed the red Avenger wrapped around a tree. That once nice paint job was now accompanied by bullets. I smiled at the job well done and headed towards my crib. Just as I turned the block, my phone rang.

"Yeah," I answered on the second ring.

"It's taken care of," the person on the other end confirmed.

"Bet," was my only response before ending the phone call.

***

I sat at a round table towards the back of the sports bar I owned in Downtown Chicago and took another shot of Henny Black. After the shit that had happened this morning, it had a motherfucker thinking. Beef was something common in the streets, but for normal niggas, and that was something I was not. That was the main reason I had called a meeting tonight: I needed to make sure everyone on my team had their ears to the streets. In the meantime, Smoke was meeting me here so we could discuss business. This nigga was always running late for whatever reason. Just when I reached for my phone to send him a text, he walked in the door.

"Nigga, you sitting in the back with the lights all dimmed like you a Mob boss or some shit," Smoke said, walking towards me.

"Bitch-ass nigga, I am a boss. What up?" I replied.

"Shit, I can't call it. I heard some niggaz came through shooting at you like Big Worm did to Smokey and Craig," he joked.

I laughed at this clown-ass nigga before getting serious.

"I have no idea who it was, but I better have some answers by tonight," I replied.

Smoke and I went over a few more details about a shipment we had coming in in a few days. He spoke briefly about how he wanted to start a couple new business ventures, and just as we started to discuss expanding our ˙ blocks out West, my phone rang.

"What's up, Bossman?" I answered.

"What's up, son? What's going on?" Quincy Taylor replied.

"Business as usual. Smoke and I was just talking about our next move."

"That's the shit I like to hear. I hadn't heard from you in a few days, so I had to make sure you were good," Quincy stated.

"I'm straight, old man, what you been up to?" I asked.

"Ya know, staying young. Fucking these bitches and getting money," he laughed.

"Yeah, a'ight. Tamika gon' kick yo' ass," I played along.

Quincy and Quintin were in their early fifties but acted as if they were my age. They both had a young soul, and that was why I fucked with them so heavy.

Quincy and I talked for about ten more minutes. Once I got off the line with him, I redirected my attention back to Smoke and the initial conversation we were having.

"How long you been knowing the Taylor twins, bruh?" he asked out the blue.

I looked over at my right-hand man and shook my head. I knew exactly where this conversation was going. "Bruh, we been through this already, but since I was younger, why?" I quizzed.

"And you really trust them?" he shot back.

"Why wouldn't I? They've made both of us rich. I would think you'd trust them, too."

"I'm saying, though, they seem so secretive. You've known them all this time, and you've never even been to their crib. How much do you really know about these muthafuckers?" he asked.

"Maaaannnn, listen, as long as I'm getting paid, I can give two fucks about an invite to dinner. And if I was the head of a cartel with a wife and kids, motherfuckers wouldn't know where I lived either. You focused on the wrong shit, bruh," I said, taking another shot of Henny.

Just as he was about to respond, the doors to the bar swung open, and in walked Mocha and her girlfriend, Courtney. It had slipped my mind that fast that she was stopping by to drop off a package for us.

"What's up, y'all? Fuck y'all on, some mob shit?" she asked, looking around.

"I told you. I told you," Smoke said, laughing.

I couldn't help but laugh myself; they were both dumb as hell.

"Here, boy," Mocha said, handing Smoke a huge, yellow manila folder filled with money.

Smoke looked inside, then slid it across the table to me.

"Nice doing business with you, hoe," Smoke laughed.

Mocha slapped him across the back of the head. "So, what y'all end up doing after the club last night?" she asked.

"Shit, I went to the crib," Smoke said.

"Yeah, me too," I followed.

"What about y'all? Y'all strapped each other?" Smoke asked, looking back and forth between Mocha and her girl.

"You a loser, but naw, we chilled with Princess at the hospital for a minute and then—"

"Aye, how her kid doing?" I asked, cutting her off.

"She's good, hard-headed as fuck, but good," Courtney answered.

"Straight up," I said, laughing.

I wanted to ask more about shorty right then and there, but I didn't want to sound thirsty. I figured if I ran into her again, then that was when I'd shoot my shot.

"A'ight, y'all, we finna slide. I'll get up with y'all later," Mocha said, grabbing her purse off the table.

"Nice meeting y'all again," Courtney said, following Mocha.

The two of them made their way out. They were both fine as fuck, but they didn't have shit on Princess. I couldn't tell you the last time a chick left a lasting impression on me. I knew I said I'd catch up with her another time, but fuck that.

"Aye, yo, Courtney, let me holler at you before you

dip out!" I yelled to the front of the bar before they made their way out the door.

If I wanted shorty, I had to make my move now. I'd hate for another nigga to slide in, then I'd have to kill him.

PRINCESS

I looked down at the rose gold Rolex watch that rested on my right arm and read the time. It was 11:30 a.m. and my last interviewer was scheduled to be here at 11:45 a.m. This was my fourth interview this morning, and I hoped and prayed I saw something in this last person that I hadn't seen in the other three. Courtney always insisted I do the interviews because she claimed that I was sterner than she was, but truth be told, I think she gets lazy and tired and would just hire any-fucking-body.

Beep.

"Ms. Taylor, your last interview has arrived," Megan, the receptionist, announced through the speakerphone.

"Thanks, Megan, send him in."

I grabbed the folder that held Mr. Brooks resume and looked over it one more time. This man really had a strong background and had worked for some impressive companies.

"Good luck, Mr. Brooks," I heard Megan say before my eyes peered away from the papers in front of me to the person standing in front of my desk.

"You know they say you shouldn't arrive more than ten minutes early for an interview, I think I'm good," JA said, looking over at the clock on the wall of my office.

I couldn't believe my eyes, and I was speechless, something that didn't happen often. I never took him as the type to do construction, and what were the odds of him interviewing for a position at my company. Something seemed off.

"Can I have a seat?" he asked, gesturing towards the chair.

"I'm…I'm sorry. I'm a little thrown off. Please, have a seat," I replied, lifting from my seat a little as he sat down.

"So, Mr. Brooks, tell me about yourself," I continued, snapping back into interview mode.

"Well, I'm a Leo, Jay-Z is my favorite rapper, my favorite color is blue, annnnddd, ummmm, I love Flamin' Hots," he said, smiling, rubbing his hands across his beard.

Everything about this man made my pussy moist: his smile, that one dimple that invaded his cheek, the way he wore those navy-blue slacks and Versace shirt, those colorful tattoos that seemed to stand out on his light skin like it was in 3D.

"Mr. Brooks, all that's cool, but tell me something about you that relates to the position," I finally replied.

"How about you tell me more about yourself, Ms. Taylor," he said with a smirk.

"Well, I'm the one interviewing you, so I'll ask the questions," I shot back.

"It's been a while since I been on an interview, but I thought they encouraged you to ask questions. Ya know, make it seem like you really care about the company or what not," he replied.

I couldn't help but smile this time. "Mr. Brooks—"

"Call me JA." He cut me off.

"Well, I like to keep things as professional as

possible, so I'll stick to Mr. Brooks," I assured him.

"So, does that mean no dating in the workplace?" he asked.

"That's exactly what that means," I guaranteed him.

JA looked at me, licking his lips before standing and walking towards the door.

"Well, I do apologize for wasting your time, Ms. Taylor, but I rather have you as my woman than have you as my boss."

JA had me open. I'd never been this impressed before, maybe because I had never given a nigga the time of day, but he had me reconsidering.

"JA," I called out to him before he left out the door.

"What's up, baby?" he responded, turning around halfway.

"Come here, I got a question," I said, motioning for him to come to me with my index finger.

JA laughed a little before turning around, closing the door behind him. He slowly walked over towards my desk, and all I could think about was him laying on this Cherry Oakwood desk, and me riding his dick. He stopped in front of me and just stood there, waiting for me to say whatever it was I had to say, but truthfully, I didn't know. I just didn't want him to leave.

"I have a few more interviews to do, then I need to consult with my partner before making a decision, I'll be in touch," I said, winking my right eye.

"You know what, I'll pass. You be having wet

dreams and shit about me already. I can see us ending up in court, going through some sexual harassment shit. This can get ugly," he said, laughing before walking out my office.

***

"BITCH, I CAN'T BELIEVE YOU TOLD HIM THAT!" I screamed, punching Courtney in the arm.

Courtney bent over in my closet, holding her stomach, laughing uncontrollably, but I didn't find shit funny.

"I should beat yo' ass. Why you tell that man about the dream I had about him?" I asked, followed by me placing her in a headlock.

"Princess, 'cause he asked. He was like, 'What yo' cousin been up to?' and I let it slip," she replied, still giggling.

"How you let that slip?" I asked, releasing her.

"I was just like, 'She been cool, having wet dreams about you and shit.' Nothing major, Princess, so chill."

"Chill? Hoe, that's embarrassing," I whined.

"It can't be too embarrassing, you are getting dressed to go out with him right now," Courtney chuckled.

"Girl, whatever. Shut up."

I threw a pillow at her before stepping into my low-rise, ripped Gucci jeans. I wore an all-white Gucci crop top to match with a pair of slide-in Gucci heel sandals. I touched up my makeup a little before Courtney applied edge control to my runaway baby hairs.

"You so bad, cousin," Courtney complimented as I looked myself over in the full-length mirror.

"Thanks, gay-gay," I replied, blowing her an air kiss, which she caught.

I grabbed my phone off the charger on the nightstand, along with my favorite Gucci clutch, and headed towards the door.

"Harmony, I'll be back, call me if you need anything!" I yelled, walking past my daughter's bedroom.

"Wait. Wait. Wait, mommy, let me see you. You know I gotta approve!" Harmony yelled, running out the door.

I stopped dead in my tracks and rolled my eyes. My ten-year-old had a way of being brutally honest, and too fucking blunt at times.

"OK. OK. OK. Give me a full spin," she said, motioning with her finger for me to twirl around.

I did as I was instructed while Courtney watched and laughed from the upstairs balcony.

"Mama, you so dope. Now knock 'em dead," she said, giving me a fist pump.

I was actually relieved because truth be told, had she not approved of my outfit, I would have carried my black ass back upstairs to change.

I gave my daughter a kiss and told her I loved her before heading to the restaurant to meet JA. He insisted on picking me up, but I think explaining to him how I'm the daughter of a cartel boss might be too much for a first date, so I came up with a lie about not wanting a nigga to know where I lived so soon. I mean, it was partially the truth.

I arrived downtown in about thirty minutes, and he sent me the address to a rooftop restaurant right off of Michigan Ave. When I pulled up, the street was empty and quiet, which was strange, especially for it to be the heart of downtown. Usually, there would be blustering people everywhere you turned. I stopped my car, and a valet attendant with a bouquet of roses greeted me.

"These are for you, and I'll take your keys."

I smiled and thanked him before heading into the restaurant. I stopped at the door when I noticed a note with my name on it. "*Follow the rose petals*," was all it read. I placed the note in my clutch and followed the instructions given to me.

"I know this nigga did not have this restaurant shut down for our date," I said to myself as I made my way up the final flight of stairs.

My suspicions were confirmed when I walked through the glass doors, and he stood over by the table, waiting for me with another bouquet of roses. Instead, these were my favorite, Rosa Peace.

"Hey, beautiful." He greeted me with a tight hug.

This was the first time in a long time I'd had this type of embrace. The smell of his Tom Ford Black cologne danced around in my nostrils. His strong arms wrapped around my body made me wish time would freeze. I didn't want this moment to end, but I also didn't want to be a creep, so I released first.

"You look nice," I said to him as he pulled out my chair for me.

"Aw, this is nothing," he replied, brushing me off.

Ironically, he wore a tan Gucci jacket, that he had left open, with a plain white shirt underneath, a pair of stone-washed jeans, and loose laced Timbs. Contrary to the first time I had met him, he kept it simple tonight with only one diamond chain and bracelet. He looked to have just stepped out of the barbershop chair because his fade and beard lining was on point. I was always doubtful when it came to men, but I prayed he acted right, at least for one night because I'd hate to fuck him and leave.

JA

Either she the one or I'm caught in the matrix. I recited a Jay-Z lyric in my head while staring at Princess, sitting across the table from me. It had been so long since I'd been on a date, and with the help of her cousin, Courtney, it was easy pulling it off. She told me Princess' favorite food as well as her favorite roses so I could be better prepared.

"Can I get you two anything to drink?" the waiter said, joining us at the table.

I waited for Princess to place her drink order, then I followed, ordering just a Sprite.

"So, you really shut the place down for our date, huh? I'm impressed." She smiled at me.

"Well, anything for MY Princess," I replied, winking my right eye.

Princess looked at me, trying her hardest not to blush, but she couldn't help it. The crazy thing about it all was, I forever wanted to continue to make her blush.

"So, JA, tell me a little about yourself," she said, changing the subject.

"Well, shid, honestly, I'm just a man trying to see a couple of million before I die," I replied truthfully.

"Come on now, there has to be more to you than that," she responded.

"Nah, on some real shit, my pops died in a car accident when I was younger. He left my OG and little sister enough paper to make it through life for a few years. I took my bread when I turned twenty-one and invested, later opening a little bar I got downtown and the car dealership I got with Smoke's ass," I semi-lied.

Telling her the truth would have her looking at me funny. I couldn't open up about my pops being a known killer in the hood with two best friends who were now drug lords. That shit only sounded right in books. I at least had to feel her out first.

"Shit, I'm sorry to hear about your pops. How old is your little sister?" she asked.

"Her crazy ass is seventeen. She a senior at Naperville North High School."

"Awwwww, I always wanted a little sister," she replied.

"Ah, you the only child, that explains a lot," I admitted.

Princess looked at me and turned up her nose. "And what the fuck that supposed to mean? But yeah, I'm the only child. Courtney is the closest thing I have to a sister."

"Courtney cool as fuck, but your turn, what's your story?" I shot back.

"Well, my mom is a lawyer and my father is a doctor. As you know, I have a ten-year-old daughter, and I used the money my parents saved up for me to go to college to open my strip club and construction company," she stated.

"Awwww, li'l trust fund baby, huh?" I joked.

"Yo' ugly ass just tried it," she laughed, tossing a piece of bread at me from the basket the waiter had brought to the table.

After we ordered our food, we engaged in more conversation, and before I knew it, it was almost one in the morning. Princess talked a little more about herself and her daughter, and we both discussed how hectic it was running our own businesses. What turned me on the most was that she was a basketball fan. We argued about Lebron James and Steph Curry, even placing a bet on who would win the finals. Although it was late, it was evident that neither one of us wanted to leave.

"So, look, right, the gentleman in me wants to make sure you make it home safe, but the JA in me don't wanna see you leave," I confessed.

Princess placed her right hand over her heart. "That was the sweetest shit you've said to me all night," she replied.

"I know you lying, I been hitting you with some of my best game," I joked.

"Well, ya game weak, my dude. Sorry to be the one to tell you that, but it is time for me to go," she said, standing.

Her body was shaped like a Coco-Cola bottle. She had the smallest waist, but her hips were wide as fuck. I couldn't help but stare.

"Well, since I can't make sure you make it home safely because you secretive and shit about yo' address, the least I can do is walk you down to your car," I replied, finally standing up as well.

"A gentleman and a thug, I like that," she said, winking her right eye at me.

I walked around the table to her side and grabbed

her hand, locking her fingers with mine before we walked off the patio. Her hands were so soft, it almost wigged me out. I hadn't held hands with a woman since... never. Once we made it outside, I stood behind her closely while we waited for the valet to bring her car around. He pulled up and handed her the keys before going on about his business.

"So, Mr. Brooks, I enjoyed our date, the food was amazing, and so was your company and conversation," she said, turning around, facing me.

"Well, I'm glad you enjoyed yourself, and I hope this won't be our last date," I replied, grabbing her by the waist, pulling her close to me.

I could smell the stick of Doublemint gum that she had placed into her mouth moments ago as she looked at me and smiled. "Yeah, me either," she replied, leaning forward on her tiptoes, placing a soft kiss on my lips. I couldn't lie, that little peck had a nigga slightly mesmerized. I wasn't even the kissing type, but she made me want more.

"Goodnight," she announced, walking off from me and towards her car, but I grabbed her by the jacket she wore tied around her waist before she could make it far.

"Aye, man, stop playing wit' me," was all I said before kissing those soft lips again, this time, allowing my tongue to intertwine with hers once she parted her lips.

"Call me when you make it home," I requested, finally letting her go.

"How about you call me now, and we talk until I make it home," she replied, hopping in her car.

"Say no more."

I pulled out my phone from my pocket, went to my contacts, and dialed her number. We talked the forty-five-minute drive it took for her to get home. That call leaked over until about six in the morning, and shorty had a nigga feeling like he was in high school again.

PRINCESS

"OK, cousin, I see you! A bitch losing weight, ass getting fat, face clearing up and girrrrlllll, is those yo' edges growing back?" Courtney said, sitting across the dining room table from me at my parents' house.

"Shut up, bitch, before they hear you," I said through clenched teeth as I kicked her under the table.

"OK, bitch, annnddddd... you acting like you twelve. You can't date? What the fuck? Shid, Harmony about to starting dating in a minute and you hiding your relationship," she shot back.

"Lower your voice, and it ain't a relationship," I replied.

"Girl, what you call it? You and JA been spending damn near every day together for the past two weeks. Ohhhhh, I get it, you ain't fucked yet, so it's not a relationship. Is that it?" she quizzed.

Courtney was irritating the fuck out of me, as usual, but she was right. JA and I were joined at the hip, but like I said, we were not in a relationship. Neither one of us had made things official yet. I honestly felt that we should at least get to know each other first, but I really, really liked that man, I couldn't even stunt.

"Don't worry about what's going on in my sex life. You need to—"

"What about a sex life?" my mom said, interrupting me, walking into the dining area, taking a seat.

"Nun, Ma," I replied, rolling my eyes at Courtney.

"Exactly, auntie, nothing. We all know YOUR

DAUGHTER don't have one of those," she said, referring to a sex life, throwing me under the bus.

My mom cut her eyes over at me and started laughing. "You do know when I said you bet' not never have sex again as a teenager, I only meant, as a teenager. It's OK now, Princess, you grown," my mom replied, high-fiving Courtney as they both laughed hard as hell.

"What's so funny in here?" my dad asked, walking up with my Uncle Quintin and Auntie Domo in tow.

"Nothing, daddy. Nothing at all," I quickly stated before anybody else could comment.

"I know y'all not having girl talk without me," Auntie Domo chimed in.

"Nah, Ma, we were just saying how Princess all secretive about her relationship," Courtney spoke again.

Just as I was about to snap, my dad interjected, "Baby girl, you in a relationship? Really? With who? A man or a woman?" he asked in a serious tone.

"First of all, I'm talking to this MAN, and the only one munching on carpet at this table is this big head heffa right here," I said, pointing to Courtney.

"Well, she not the only one," my dad said, winking at my mom.

"Uggghhhh, come on now, daddy, I caught that," I whined.

"Yeah, like my baby brother said, I personally enjoy munching," my uncle added, looking over at my auntie.

The entire table burst out in laughter. "What's so funny, y'all?" Harmony asked, joining us at the table.

And just as quickly as the laughter started, it stopped. "Nothing, Granny baby, nothing at all. Have a seat," my mother said.

Moments later, the cooks brought the food to the table, and we all dived in. We had a family dinner once a week, and we rotated houses. Last week, we were over at my Auntie and Uncle's home, and next week, Harmony and I would be the hosts. Tonight's feast included steak, potatoes, asparagus, broccoli, garlic bread and shrimp. Walter and Mary, my parents' chefs, were the best to ever do it. I had grown up with their cooking as a child, and as an adult, I appreciated it even more.

We all fed our faces in silence, enjoying the wonderful meal. Things even stayed that way once the homemade German chocolate cake was brought out.

"Yasssss, I'm about to smash!" Harmony said excitedly as she looked on.

I looked over at my baby and laughed, then down at the table when I felt my phone vibrate. I had an unread message from JA.

JA: Shorrrtttyyyyyyyyyyyy.

ME: Lmao…. What boy?

JA: Aye meet me at my bar, I got something for you.

ME: I guess saying "please" would be a stretch.

JA: Man just do what tf I told you. See you in an hour baby.

I smiled, shook my head and locked my phone. When I looked up, everybody was staring at me, smiling.

"WHAT!" I asked, placing a fork full of cake in my mouth.

I wrapped up things at my parents' house and headed downtown to meet JA, per his request. I really wished I had time to change out of the leggings and shirt I was wearing, but I knew I would be chancing it if I did. I pulled up to "JA'S SPORTS AND BAR", found a parking space in front and hopped out. It was a Wednesday night, and the place was closed, so I had no idea why he had me meet him down here instead of at his crib.

"Hey, baby," I said, walking over to him at the bar, giving him a hug.

JA grabbed a hand full of my ass and squeezed it. "What's up, beautiful?" he replied.

"Shit, just left my parents'. We had dinner over there tonight."

"Oh yeah, I forgot The Cosbys did that shit once a week," he replied.

"It's the Huxtables, first of all, but yeah, every Wednesday night," I corrected him with a fake attitude.

Little did he know, my family was the furthest thing from the Huxtables. We were definitely more like the Sopranos, but he didn't need to know that.

"So, what's up? Why you have me meet you here?" I continued, looking around his dope-ass bar.

"DAMN! I can't wanna see my girl? That's an issue, Princess?" he replied, twisting his head to the side.

"Aw, so now I'm your girl?" I quizzed.

"Nah, not yet, I was just practicing," he laughed, going into his back pocket, pulling out an all-white envelope, handing it to me.

"What's this?" I asked, taking it from him.

"Look inside, Princess," he replied.

I rolled my eyes at him and ripped open the envelope, revealing two tickets to the NBA Finals.

"Oh my God, these tickets to the game," I said excitedly, my eyes lit up like a Christmas tree.

"Yup, courtside, baby," he boasted.

"Wait, these for us? OH MY GOD, JA!" I wrapped my arms around his neck, squeezing him tight before kissing his lips.

"But wait, the game is in California," I said, coming down from my high.

"Yeah, this Friday, so clear yo' schedule. We are flying out tomorrow night. I'll have you back Sunday morning," he ordered.

Usually, I'd protest. I hated being told what to do, but I couldn't. He wasn't wrong, and as a matter of fact, he was doing everything right.

"It's so last minute, but I guess," I smiled.

"I love that smile," he said, rubbing my chin.

"Just make sure you always keep it there," I shot back.

"It's all a part of my plan, Princess. It's all a part of my plan, baby."

JA

I stood outside Midway Airport, looking down at the gold Rolex on my arm as I waited for Princess to arrive. Our flight was leaving in an hour. I insisted on picking her up, but she declined my offer. She stated that since she was already staying with Courtney until her house was finished, Courtney wouldn't mind dropping her off. Just as I was about to shoot Smoke a text, reminding him of the business he had to uphold while I was gone, a white Mercedes truck pulled up, and Princess hopped out.

"My bad, Courtney drive like she eighty-five," she said, going to the back seat to retrieve her bags.

I laughed to myself before stepping off the curb to help her. "It's cool, what up, Courtney!" I waved to her as she sat on the driver side.

"Heeeyyyyyyy, JA!" she said in a flirty tone that caused all of us to laugh.

"I think you got what it takes to turn my cousin straight," Princess said as we walked through the airport doors.

"You think so, cuz I ain't never turned a muthafucker straight... Aye, Courtney, come back!" I yelled, turning around like I was going back to the car.

Princess playfully punched me in the arm. "Stop playing with me."

The transition from check-in through TSA went smoothly. Our flight was set to depart at 8:35 p.m., and surprisingly, the airport was damn near empty. We made it to our gate with thirty minutes to spare, so we found a seat near the window and talked.

"A'ight, so you wanna bet on game seven now or later?" I asked her.

"What's your wager, big dog?" she shot back.

"A'ight, look, so if Golden State wins, I gotta be your man, and if Lebron nem bitch ass win, then you gotta be my girl... A'ight, you cool with that, too... good."

She looked at me and started laughing. Just as she was about to speak, the flight attendant came over the loudspeaker, informing us that our group was ready to board. We gathered the little shit we had and got on the plane. The flight from Chicago to California was four hours and twelve minutes, and shorty must have had a long night because she was knocked out before we hit the air.

The flight was cool, for the most part. I dozed off a little bit after her. When we landed, I picked up my rental car, a two-seater drop top, and headed to the hotel. I had booked us a room at the Palace, which was about ten miles from Oracle Arena.

"You hungry?" I looked over at her and asked as we drove the streets of Oakland, California.

"Yeah, I can eat. What about you?" she asked, looking at me.

"Yeah, I'm hungry than a muthafucker. All the real restaurants closed, so we can order room service when we get there," I informed her.

"Nah, there go a Jack In The Box right there," she said, pointing up the street.

I cut the radio down to make sure I wasn't tweaking. "So, you want Jack In The Box?" I asked for clarity.

"Ummmm, yeah," she clarified.

I couldn't help but laugh. This girl seemed to amaze me every day. It was hard to believe that she had grown up the way she had, but she was so down to Earth.

"What the fuck is so funny?" she asked, shifting in her seat.

"Nun… Well, it's just that with your upbringing and all, I thought a place like this wouldn't be something you'd prefer," I admitted truthfully.

"Well, JA, there's a lot more to me than you know," she said in a low tone before looking out the window.

I wasn't sure what she meant by her statement, and I wasn't the type of nigga to pry, so I figured when she was ready, we would discuss further details then.

We got our burgers, fries and drinks and headed to check in at the hotel.

"You want your food now, or you gon' wait till we get to the room?" she asked, crunching on a fry she had stolen from the bag.

"I mean, I was gon' wait cuz I'm driving, but a nigga hungry now," I replied, looking at the road.

My eyes darted over to Princess when I heard the bags rumbling. She pulled out my burger, began to unwrap it for me, then said, "Here, bite," holding it to my mouth as I hopped on the highway.

We drove in silence, minus a few smacks from the food and slurps from the pop we were drinking. She fed me and fed herself, finishing up just as I pulled into the parking lot of the hotel. I got the bags out the trunk, and we both went to the front desk to check in.

"Hey, I got a reservation for Brooks," I said, handing the young lady at the receptionist desk my ID.

She looked at me smiling before typing some information into the computer and handing my card back to me.

"Thanks so much, Mr. Brooks. Will there be any special requests? You need extra pillows or towels? A later check out time Sunday? A wakeup call? I can personally come and wake you up myself," she said with a flirty grin.

"NAH, BITCH, HE GOOD!" Princess snapped, snatching the key cards out of her hands before turning and walking away.

"I'm sorry about that, ma'am—"

"JA, bring yo' friendly ass ON!" she yelled from the elevator.

I laughed and grabbed the bags, walking over to an awaiting Princess. We took the elevator to the twelfth floor where our penthouse was located. I made sure that I spared no expenses when it came to our mini-vacation, but I had to keep in mind that I was a "businessman" and not the hustler I really was, so I toned shit down a little.

"Got damn, JA, you do know it's just me and you, right? A simple suite wouldn't have sufficed?" she asked, looking around the huge living area.

"Nah, I'm not a simple nigga, remember that," I replied, walking by her, stealing a kiss.

We both looked around a little before settling in the bedroom, and Princess wasted no time jumping in the shower. It was almost one in the morning, three if we were still in the central time zone, so I knew she was just as tired as I was. She spent about twenty minutes in the bathroom while I chilled across the bed, watching SportsCenter. I felt myself dozing off when the bathroom doors opened, and she walked out wearing nothing but a towel.

"Damn, shorty," I said, licking my lips, walking close to her, kissing her on the neck.

She squealed and fought me off. "Nah, go get yo' musty ass in the shower," she said, pushing me towards the bathroom.

"Damn, for real?" I replied, lifting my arms, sniffing myself as she laughed.

"Yeah, I knew yo' ass was lying, but I'ma get in the shower anyway," I said, slamming the bathroom door, leaving her standing there alone.

I got the water to the perfect temperature before hopping in, and I searched for my soap, realizing I had left it in the bedroom.

"Fuck," I said to myself.

I knew if I used the complimentary soap that came with the room, that shit was going to dry my skin out and I was going to be walking around this bitch musty for real.

"AYE, PRINCESS!!" I yelled out to her so she could bring my soap, but she never answered.

"Fuck it," I said, grabbing her soap. It was some shit called "Beautiful Day" from Bath & Body Works, but the shit smelled good.

I lathered up my towel and washed my body a few

times before rinsing off, drying off, and exiting the steamy bathroom.

I tied the towel around the lower half of my body and stepped out into the empty, freezing, air-conditioned room. I figured Princess would be sleep by now, so I was a bit shocked watching her over at the bar located in the living area, knocking back shots.

"Damn, you good?" I asked, walking over to where she was.

She looked up at me and smiled. "I'm straight. Come take a shot with me," she replied, pouring some Henny into a shot glass and sliding it across the bar to me.

I lifted the glass in the air, signaling for a toast before I knocked it back. "Ahhhhh," I grunted at the strong taste of the alcohol.

"That shit would put hair on ya chest," she said, sliding me another shot glass.

"What, you trying to get me drunk and take advantage of me?" I asked, downing my second shot.

She looked at me and smirked. "Boy, please, you going either way it go," she replied, smiling.

"You damn right!" I assured her, walking around to where she was standing. Grabbing the loose end of the towel she was wearing, I yanked it.

She allowed the towel to fall, revealing a perfect body underneath before she walked over to me, unraveling my towel. I noticed her eyes buck when she got the first glance at my dick. Before she could react, I grabbed her, kissing her, using my tongue to explore her mouth. I reached down and started playing with her hardened nipples as she moaned in between our kisses. I then took my hands, traveling further south, where I discovered her wet spot. I took my index finger and massaged her clit as she became weak in the knees. I lifted her into the air, sliding the liquor to one side of the bar with my free hand, sitting her on top of the bar. I then opened her legs wider and dived in. Princess tasted so sweet, it was as if I was feasting on one of my favorite meals. I used my tongue to massage her clit in a circular motion, and I could tell from the way she was screaming and moaning, she was enjoying it. And, by the way my dick grew, I was enjoying it, too.

"Oh my God, JA, I'm about to cuuuummmmm!" she yelled at the top of her lungs as her legs shook, her sweetness filling my mouth.

I picked her up from the bar, placing her back on the floor. I pulled a stool in front of her and leaned her body forward, positioning her so I had the perfect back angle. I then played with her pussy a little more, getting it wetter before I slid in. Now, I was not one hundred percent sure I had ever taken someone's virginity back in my younger days, but I swear to God, it felt like I was taking hers, that was how tight she was.

"Just relax," I whispered to her as I felt her body relax a little.

I took my time and went in, feeling her walls stretch with each inch I put inside her. I started off slow, just to make sure she was good, but when she started throwing it back and moaning louder and louder, I picked up the pace. Her pussy was the best I'd ever had, and I had to start thinking about shit like my dead relatives in order to not cum, but even that shit didn't work.

"Babbbbyyyy, I'm cumming again," she moaned,

and those were the words I'd been waiting to hear.

"Me too, baby," I replied, going deeper and deeper inside of her. Seconds later, we both reached our peak.

PRINCESS

"Sex game have that ass blowing me up. Sex game have that ass texting me up. I got the moves. I got the moves..."

I pulled the covers over my head and giggled. JA's irritating ass had been singing that same song all morning, taunting me. I should have never told him how good his dick was, but I couldn't help it. His already big-ass head grew bigger when I fucked up and told him he was the only dude I'd fucked in the last ten years. If he didn't already think he was the man, he was sure of it now.

"I thought we was gon' do some sightseeing today?" JA said, walking out of the bathroom.

"I did tooooo, but now I don't want to get out the bed. Well, at least not until the game," I whined.

"So, you know why you can't get out the bed, right?" he replied, crawling back under the covers with me.

I shook my head and rolled my eyes. "Nah, JA, I don't know why. Care to tell me?" I asked sarcastically.

"It's cuz... I GOT THE MOVES! I GOT THE MOVES!"

I hit JA upside the head with one of the pillows nearest to me before he grabbed me, pinning me down on the bed, staring into my eyes.

"What?" I questioned, staring directly into his.

"You look familiar as fuck. You sure I ain't never fuck you before?" he asked, but lowkey, I knew he was dead serious.

"Nah, fool, and trust me, you would remember that," I replied, still pinned under him.

"Shorty, yo' pussy decent and all, but it ain't like its unforgettable or no shit like that," he smiled.

"Now, head... head is something I don't forget, so ummmmmmmm, Princess, you got a good head on your shoulders or what?" he continued.

This man kept me laughing, and that was just one of the many things I adored about him, but I had to keep shit 100 with him.

"I ain't never gave head before," I admitted honestly.

"WHAT? Man, quit playing... Oh, wait, you dead ass, huh?" he said, realizing I was being truthful.

I lowered my head, looking away from his stares.

"Princess, it's a'ight," he said, lifting my chin. "It ain't even that deep, shorty," he continued.

"Bruh, it's definitely that deep. How many twenty-five-year-old women you know ain't never sucked dick?" I asked.

"NONE... And that's why I fucks with you even more," he replied, sitting up.

"Yeah, but that's the very reason niggaz cheat: they cheat when they not satisfied."

"Niggaz cheat cuz we want to. You can be sucking the skin off a motherfucker dick, but if he wants to dip out, then that's what he gon' do."

I knew JA was being truthful, and I appreciated that, but him saying what he said hadn't put my mind to ease, it just confirmed what I already knew.

"A'ight, come on, man. Get up so we can do a little shopping," he said, getting off the bed. "COME ON!" he yelled when he noticed that I hadn't moved.

"Lay down, JA. I rather learn how to suck yo' dick than shop right now," I said seductively.

JA stopped midair and turned around to face me. "Come again," he said with a look of confusion on his face.

I giggled before repeating myself, although I knew he had already heard me. "I said, I rather learn how to suck yo' dick than shop," I repeated.

A smile as wide as the Grinch's spread across his face. "Shiiiiddddd, you ain't gotta tell me twice," he said, pulling off the wife beater he was wearing and stepping out of the Hanes briefs that were once on his body.

I couldn't control my laughter. He was moving at top speed, and before I knew it, he was standing on the side of the bed, asshole naked and ashy.

"Why are you so silly?" I asked, still unable to control my laughter.

"See, I knew you was playing," he replied, reaching for his clothes.

"No. No. No. Come here. I'm serious," I said, sitting up and scooting over to the edge of the bed.

I admired his long, light dick, and even IT was pretty. This nigga turned me on in every way imaginable.

"Look, you don't have to—GOOOOOTTTTTT DAMMMMMNNNN, Princess."

His whole demeanor changed once I placed his dick into my mouth. Now, don't get me wrong, I'd watched enough porn to know the basics of sucking dick, I just was the furthest thing from a pro.

"Damn, a'ight… you gotta get yo' mouth wet as possible. Remember, the wetter, the better," he coached.

I remember seeing a video when the lady said that gagging on it would create more saliva, so that was what I did, but I think I went too far because my eyes started watering. However, JA must have been enjoying it.

"You doing good, baby. The objective is to make your mouth feel like—GOOOTTTT DAMMMMNN!" he exclaimed.

The more I sucked his dick, the wetter my pussy got. This shit was turning me on something crazy.

"So, how am I doing?" I stopped to ask.

"Rule number one, less talking and more sucking… but you doing good, baby. Keep going."

His little speech was encouraging for me, so I sucked his dick and played with his balls occasionally until he came.

"Aye, aye, aye, back up, bae, I'm finna cum," he moaned, pulling his body back, but I pulled him closer, placing his dick back into my mouth, catching all he had to offer and swallowing it.

The look of shock on his face was worth capturing. Hell, I had shocked myself. I had no intention of swallowing my first time giving head, but I liked to be the best at whatever I did.

"Females love hitting niggaz with the *'I never did this before'* line, then turn around and take they soul," he said, walking into the bathroom.

I laughed because he wasn't lying, but neither was I. "Boy, shut the fuck up and get ready for this game," I replied, throwing the remote at him as he disappeared into the bathroom.

My love for basketball was electrifying, and sitting courtside, being able to touch Lebron James if I just extended my arm, was driving me crazy. I was pretty sure I was the only one wearing a Cavs jersey surrounded by a sea of blue and yellow, but I couldn't care less. I was a true fan.

JA and I enjoyed the game as well as each other's company. It was all fun and laughter until the fourth quarter when the game clock read fifty-seven seconds with Cleveland up by five points. All the Golden State fans clutched their invisible pearls while I, on the other hand, was happier than a kid in the candy store.

Buzz...

The final buzzer sounded, and like I'd been hollering since October, the Cleveland Cavaliers were victorious this season. I looked around at the sad faces displayed on Golden State's fans, then I turned to the left of me and saw the saddest face of them all.

"Nigga, run me my monneyyy," I said, impersonating Smokey off the movie *Friday*.

JA looked at me side-eyed. "Man, shut the fuck up,

we ain't bet no money. They ass cheated, calling all those unnecessary-ass fouls."

"Womp, womp, womp. You sound like the teacher on Charlie Brown. Y'all always crying that cheating shit when they win. Shut yo' punk ass up," I snapped, shoving him in the face with my index finger.

"I'ma fuck you up, come here," he said, pulling me close to him.

"What?" I asked, poking out my bottom lip, taunting him.

He wrapped his arms around my waist before speaking. "You know this only mean one thing, right?"

"Oh, and what is that?" I questioned.

"My team lost, so you gotta be my girl," he said, biting his bottom lip. And that was how the story of Princess and JA began.

SECOND QUARTER

PRINCESS

Two months later

I laid across my king-sized bed and stared at the ceiling. I had to have some type of bad luck. I must have broken a mirror or two because I was cursed. It was either that or sex just didn't agree with me. I felt like fourteen-year-old Princess again, asking God where I had gone wrong. What were the odds that the two times out of my life I'd had sex, I'd get pregnant both the times? Through the years, when I'd been with guys, it had been strictly oral, no penetration at all, and then here comes JA, sticking his big-ass dick in me, and now I was pregnant.

This morning, I took two tests, and both of them had come back positive. If my calculations were correct, I should be almost nine weeks. I got my last period two weeks before we went to California, and according to this app on my phone, I was definitely ovulating that weekend of the NBA finals. Outside of being pregnant, life was great, I guess. Both of my businesses were booming, Harmony was making straight A's, and JA and I were tighter than either one of us would have thought. I really cared about him, and sometimes I found myself questioning if I loved him, but it had only been two months since we'd made things official, and there were still a lot of secrets I kept from him.

As far as JA knew, my parents were a doctor and lawyer, lie number one, and my place was still being renovated, so I was living with Courtney, and that was why he hadn't been over to my place, lie number two. I hadn't even allowed him to meet Harmony yet. I felt it was too soon, and I didn't think it was fair to her to bring JA into her life. If things didn't work out between him and I, then what? I wasn't trying to confuse her. Outside of my father and uncle, she'd never had another male figure around.

"Girl, what's the damn emergency?" Courtney yelled, running into my room like a bat out of hell.

I had texted her ten minutes ago and told her to come over and that it was an emergency. After she texted back, questioning me, I purposely stopped replying. I knew her ass would come running then.

"Princess, what the fuck is the emergency?" she asked again, out of breath.

"Go look in the bathroom on the sink," I instructed.

She looked at me weirdly before slowly walking into the bathroom. I counted down from ten and just like I expected, she screamed.

"AHHHHHHHHHHHHHHHHHHHHHHHHHHHHH H! OH MY GOD, PRINCESS!" She ran out of the bathroom with the pregnancy applicator in her hand.

I sat up in the middle of the bed, shaking my head. "I know, I can't believe it, either."

"Wait, when did this happen? How did this happen? Did you tell JA? Bitch, I can't believe this!" she yelled.

I sat there trying to put everything into perspective myself. "It happened in Oakland. We never used protection, and nah, I haven't told him yet. I just took the test this morning," I answered.

Courtney calmed down a little before taking a seat on the bed. "So, what you gon' do?" she asked in a more serious tone.

"I mean, how many options do I have? I didn't get

rid of Harmony, and I gave birth to her when I turned fifteen. It would be selfish of me to get an abortion now," I replied, shrugging.

"You are absolutely right, I just can't believe the luck you have."

"Yeah, me either," I said in a low tone.

Courtney and I talked a little more about the pregnancy situation as well as things concerning our businesses before she left. I made her promise not to tell Mocha because I knew it would get back to JA, and I needed to be the one to tell him.

"Speaking of the devil," I said to myself as I reached for my ringing phone.

"Hello," I answered.

"What up, li'l ugly, what you doing?" JA's voice vibrated in my ears.

"Nothing, laying in the bed."

"Why, Princess? I thought you was coming over my OG's crib for Skylar's trunk party," he replied.

"I am, baby. I'm about to hop in the shower now. Did you pick up her gift yet?" I questioned.

"Yeah, I got it this morning. I need you to meet me at my crib, so one of us can drive my car, and the other person can drive Sky's new truck," he explained.

"A'ight, I'll be there, give me an hour," I said before ending the call.

I finally pulled myself out of bed, showered and

dressed like I had promised. It was the middle of August, and hot as fuck outside, so I decided to wear a fitted maxi dress that I had ordered online from Fashion Nova. I pulled my long hair back into a ponytail, put my Prada shades on and headed out the door. Harmony and a few friends were down the street at my parents' house, playing in the pool. I thought about stopping there to let her know I was gone but decided not to. I'd call her once I got in the car.

After hanging up with Harmony, I stopped at Walmart and put $1,500 on a gift card for JA's little sister, then went to his house to meet him. When I pulled up, he and Smoke were standing outside, talking and smoking.

"What's up, y'all!" I walked up, greeting them.

"What's up, baby?" JA said first.

"What's up, baby!" Smoke said, walking over, giving me a hug.

I laughed at Smoke as he purposely aggravated JA. "Nigga, you better stop playing with me," JA said, pulling me away from Smoke's embrace and into his arms.

"You look beautiful," JA said, complimenting me.

"AS ALWAYS!" Smoke added in, causing us both to laugh.

I stood off to the side while they wrapped things up when I noticed a black Maxima come around the block twice. The windows were tinted, so it was hard to make out who was inside.

"Aye, y'all, a black Maxima keeps bending the block with dark tints," I informed them when I noticed the car one final time.

"Awwww, shit," Smoke said, shaking his head.

I was about to ask what was going on when the sound of screeching brakes muted me. That same Maxima was now parked in front of JA's house. A few seconds later, a female hopped out with long, blonde braids, looking like Craig's girlfriend on *Friday*. I stood there, minding my business because I'd been around Smoke enough to know that this man fucked with all kinds of bitches, so one of them popping up on him was no surprise.

"JA, I SWEAR TO GOOOODDDDD," were the first words that left the young lady's mouth, causing my antennas to go up immediately.

I quickly secured my phone in my purse, setting it down on the porch before walking over to where they were standing.

"JA, I'M TIRED OF PLAYING WITH YOU. WHY THE FUCK YOU KEEP IGNORING ALL MY CALLS AND SHIT?" the bitch questioned.

"Look, Tika, I need you to get the fuck from over here," JA replied, looking over at me.

Tika. Tika. Tika. I repeated the name over and over again in my head. That was the name of the chick from the club the night Harmony had her allergic reaction. I remembered her walking up, talking crazy. This bitch had made me crack the screen on my phone. I walked closer to where the two of them were standing, ready to make my presence known.

"Ummmm, Tika," I said, clearing my throat, tapping her on her shoulder.

She snapped her neck around, damn near hitting me

in the face with those raggedy-ass braids.

"Bitch, who the fuck are you?" she asked.

"Remember about, ummm, let's say four months ago, I seen you at Calvin's club, on opening night. You walked up, talking crazy, and I left 'cause of some other shit. None of that is important right now, BUT I will tell you what is important. That night, I made a promise that I have to keep because I'm a woman of my word, ain't that right, baby?" I said, glancing over at JA.

"That night I told you that if I EVERRRRRRR seen you again, I was going to beat yo' ass, and now I guess... I gotta beat yo' ass," I continued. Stepping back a little, I swung on her, my right hook connecting with the bridge of her nose, causing it to leak instantly. I followed with a left hook that met with the other side of her face. I could tell that both blows had caught her off guard because she had yet to swing back, so I took advantage and rushed her with more punches.

"PRINCESS, STOP!" JA yelled, pulling me off Tika as Smoke grabbed Tika, helping her off the ground.

"BITCH, IF I EVER CATCH YOU AROUND MY MAN AGAIN, NEXT TIME, IT'S GON' BE A BULLET!" I yelled as JA carried me inside his house.

"A bullet, though, Princess. Who raised you?" JA laughed, sitting me on the couch, but I was too mad to answer him. I had questions.

"Who is she, Javaris?" I questioned.

"Come on now, you serious?" he asked.

"Serious than a motherfucker. This the second time I've encountered this bitch, and nigga, it ain't been by no coincidence," I snapped.

JA let out a loud sigh before leaning against the wall. "Look, I used to fuck with her before I met you. I got her pregnant a year ago. She killed my baby, so I stopped fucking with her," he explained.

Hearing that this bitch once carried his baby, and by the look in his eyes, her having an abortion still hurt him, hurt me.

"So, you were in love with her?" I had to ask.

"Hell nah, I wasn't. She was cool and all, but wasn't no love, baby," he replied.

"Oh," I said, lowering my head.

JA walked over to the couch and took a seat next to me. "Princess, I'm finna be real with you... ain't no bitch around can take yo' place. Your spot in my life, in my heart, is solidified."

His words made me want to cry. I could tell he was genuine, and honestly, I felt the same way about him.

JA

I drove to my OG's crib in silence, thinking about what had just happened back at my house. If Princess were one of those insecure-ass females, that stunt Tika had pulled might have scared her away. I for sure didn't expect her to beat her ass like she had, but it made me think back to what Mocha had said to me that night in the car. She was so shocked by how Princess had handled Tika at the club by staying calm, and I should have known then my girl was missing a few screws.

I looked out the rearview mirror to make sure Princess was keeping up trailing me in my car while I drove Sky's new Audi truck to her trunk party. This was my gift to her for finishing out the year on the honor roll and going off to Clark Atlanta University like I'd hoped. I couldn't lie, it was going to kill me not being able to keep an eye on her since she was going to be so far away, but I guess I couldn't win them all.

I pulled up on my mom's block, parking a few houses down just in case Sky decided to be nosy. I wanted this to be a surprise for her, and I hadn't even told my mom because she talked too much.

"You nervous?" I asked Princess once she got out of my car.

"A little," she admitted.

"You good, baby. If I love you, I know my momma will, too," I said honestly.

Princess was the first woman to ever meet my mom or my sister. The shit was kind of sad now that I thought about it. Here I was, a grown-ass man and had never been serious enough with a woman to bring her to meet my family, but better late than never, right?

The trunk party was being held in the backyard, and there were food, games, music and a bunch of teenage girls and boys everywhere. I spotted my mom and sister talking over by the grill as soon as we walked in.

"Aye, come on," I said, grabbing Princess by the hand, leading her in the direction of the two other important women in my life.

"What up, mom? What's up, big head ass little girl? This my girl, Princess. Princess, this is my mother, Joyce, and sister, Skylar," I said, introducing the three.

"Hey, nice to meet y'all," Princess said with a warm smile.

"Princess," my mom said, staring at her strangely.

It wasn't like my mom to act oddly towards people, even though she swore up and down she could get a vibe from a person in the first twenty seconds of being around them. I just hoped that she hadn't gotten one of those so-called negative vibes from Princess.

"You are soooo beautiful, give me a hug," my mom stated after examining Princess a little more.

My mother opened her arms wide, and Princess dived in.

"Aw, this is for you, and congratulations!" she said, reaching into her purse, pulling out an envelope and handing it to Sky.

"Thank you so much," Sky replied, giving Princess a hug as well.

A feeling of relief came over me. My mother's and little sister's opinion about a woman was extremely important to me, so I was glad they had taken a liking to Princess because I didn't see her going anywhere anytime soon.

After we ate, sat around, and talked for a while, it was time to open the gifts. Sky's friends had really come through for her. She wasn't staying in a dorm, but a little apartment right off campus. I had paid the rent up for a year and had vowed to continue if she kept her grades up. If not, her ass was going to need to get a job and handle the shit herself. After the last gift was given, I handed her a Tiffany & Co. box to open and inside were the keys to her new 2016 Audi truck.

"OH MY GOOODDDD, BROTHER, THANK YOUUUUU!" She jumped out of her seat and ran to where I was standing, wrapping her arms around me, kissing all over my cheek.

"A'ight. A'ight. You welcome, baby girl, and I'm proud of the woman you are becoming. Continue to make me proud, and you can get whatever you want," I replied, hugging my little sister.

Sky ran outside to look at her new whip. She drove a few of her friends around the block before continuing the celebration. While walking back to my mother's house, I noticed Princess sitting on the front porch, talking on the phone. She ended the call right after I took a seat next to her. I noticed a look of aggravation on her face, so I had to ask, "What's wrong, baby?"

"Everything's good. That was just Harmony working my last nerves, as usual," she said, looking through the phone.

"Harmony's a good child, stop acting like she's not," I spoke up.

"Yeah, you right, but she's annoying as fuck," she laughed.

"Like her momma," I added, which made her roll her eyes at me.

I loved the relationship that Princess had with her daughter. Most young mothers I knew treated their kids more like their friend, but Harmony's and Princess' relationship was a mixture of both. I couldn't wait to meet her kid. I knew she had reservations, but I didn't blame her; she had to protect her daughter by any means. And, to be honest, I was a little nervous about that anyway. I'd never dealt with a woman with children before, so I needed to prepare myself as well. I just hoped when the time did present itself, Harmony liked me.

Ring. Ring. Ring.

The sound of Princess' phone alerting her that she had an incoming FaceTime jolted me out of my personal thoughts.

"Look, a straight bug," Princess said, showing me the screen of her phone as Harmony called back.

"Yes, child," she answered.

"Awwww, mommy, you look so pretty," Harmony's soft voice said from the other end.

"Thanks, daughter, but how can I help you?"

"Where you at, Ma?" she questioned.

"Harmony, I'm out with JA. What do you want?"

she shot back.

"Ohhhhh, JA. Tell him I said hey, Ma!"

"What's up, Harmony!" I said, laughing to myself.

"How you doing, JA?" she asked.

"HARMONY… what do you want? I'm about to hang up on you!" Princess threatened.

"No, Ma. Don't hang up, listen. I wanna ask you a question. Can you pleassseeeee get me tickets to the Future concert that's coming up. Ma, please don't say no, you know I love him. He my favorite rapper, Ma. I promise I will keep my room clean and you won't have to ask me to do nothing twice. Pleaaasseeeee, mommy," Harmony begged.

"NOPE!" Princess said, ending the call, laughing.

I looked over at her, frowning. "WHAT?" she asked.

"You bogus as hell. Why the fuck you hang up on her like that?" I asked seriously.

"Because, JA, Harmony always wanting some shit."

"And you didn't at ten years old?" I shot back.

"Yeah, but…"

"But what?

"Damn, I'ma look up the tickets when I get home. You happy now?" she asked.

"Not as happy as Harmony is going to be."

PRINCESS

I never understood how symptoms didn't show until you've discovered the problem because I swear that was the case with this pregnancy. The morning after it was confirmed, I became sick as a dog. I couldn't keep anything down, my sensitivity to smell was nerve wrecking, and I promised to God if you stared at my nipples too long, they'd hurt. I didn't remember going through half of this shit when I was pregnant with Harmony, but what I did know was that eight more months of this was going to kill me.

"Princess Taylor, the doctor is ready to see you now," the young medical assistant in a blue and white smock said from the door.

I got up, grabbed my purse off the seat next to me and made my way towards her.

"How are you doing today?" she asked.

"I'm great. Thanks for asking," I replied.

That's good to hear. Dr. Wallace will be right in to see you. Oh, I almost forgot, take this; the washroom is around the corner to your left. You can leave the cup between the metal doors inside," she instructed after handing me a plastic cup to urinate in.

I took the cup and did as I was told. After I relieved myself and washed my hands, I headed back to the cold room and waited. I grabbed my phone out of my purse to look at the time; it was fifteen minutes after eleven, and I had a 10:30 appointment. I never understood the point of making appointments if you were never seen at the time scheduled. It was bad enough that I was already impatient and hungrier than a motherfucker.

Just as I was about to place my phone back in my bag, a text message came through from JA.

Bae Azz: Wya

Me: At the nail shop, waddup?

Bae Azz: How long you gon' be there?

Me: Shouldn't be no more than 30 minutes.

Bae Azz: You hungry?

Me: Lol idk how you know. I was just saying that to myself.

Bae Azz: A'ight… Meet me at Dublin's downtown.

Me: K.

A week had passed since I'd found out I was pregnant, but I still hadn't told him yet. Courtney drilled me every day, but to be honest, I was nervous. Our relationship was already moving fast, and being pregnant made the shit move at lightning speed. I guess I didn't want to scare him away, but I knew for a fact that the last thing I wanted to do was be just another baby momma.

"Well, well, well… if it isn't Ms. Taylor. I haven't seen you in forever," our family doctor, Dr. Wallace, said, entering the room.

Dr. Wallace had been our family doctor for as long as I could remember. He delivered Harmony and me, and he was the only doctor I'd ever been to.

"Hey there," I replied, standing and greeting him with a hug.

"So, how's the family been?" he questioned from the sink where he washed his hands.

"Everybody is good," I smiled.

"And that little one of yours, how is she?"

"Harmony is great, getting bigger by the second. She actually has an appointment to see you next month," I informed him.

"Great. Great. Great. I can't wait to see her. So, what brings you in today?"

I took a deep breath before coming clean. "I'm pregnant. I took two home pregnancy tests last week, and they both came back positive," I grimaced.

"Well, congratulations! You've waited long enough. When was your last period?" he inquired.

I spoke with Dr. Wallace for another fifteen minutes. He checked my vitals right before the medical assistant came in with the results, the results that I already knew.

"OK, I'm going to write out your prescription for your prenatal vitamins and for some iron pills. Go get them filled immediately, the instructions will be on the bottle. I want you to schedule a follow-up appointment with the receptionist for two weeks. I wanna hear that baby's heartbeat. You take care, and tell your mom and dad I said hello."

I thanked Dr. Wallace, but I had no plans of telling my parents that I had seen him because that would open the floodgate for more questions. But, I did do everything else he had told me to do.

After leaving the doctor's office, I stopped at Walgreens and put my prescriptions in before texting JA, letting him know I was headed to the restaurant. I called Courtney and talked to her on the ride over there, filling her in about my doctor's appointment and some work-related things. After driving for about twenty minutes and running my mouth, I pulled up right behind JA's Jaguar and parked my car. I told Courtney I'd talk to her when I got home and exited my vehicle.

"Aye, shorty!" I yelled to JA, who didn't notice I was behind him until he turned around.

He looked back with a mug before realizing it was me and stopped.

"Who the fuck still says 'Aye, shorty'?" he laughed, placing his arm around my shoulder.

"I thought y'all did. What you say to get yo' hoes?" I quizzed.

"Shidddd, honestly, I don't say shit. I just show up at their place of employment and act like I'm interviewing for a job. That drive the hoes crazy," he shot back.

I stopped walking and tilted my head to the side. "Yo' ugly ass real funny."

"You the one who wanted to know," he laughed, pushing me inside the restaurant.

Dublin's was a little bar and grill joint on State Street that had the best buffalo chicken tenders in the world. This had become mine and JA's spot on late nights or whenever we were in the vicinity. We walked in and got a table immediately and looked over the menus.

"You getting that Patrón margarita shit you always get?" JA asked, looking up briefly from his menu.

"Nah… not today. I just want a water," I lied. I didn't want a water, but I couldn't drink, considering I was with child.

Talk about timing. The waitress came to take our orders before JA had the chance to drill me more about my beverage selection.

"So, what's going on with your crib?" he asked out the blue.

"Huh? What you mean?" I replied.

"Your house, Princess. That whole renovation shit. You staying with Courtney. I'm starting to think yo' ass homeless and lying."

I cut my eyes at him before looking back down at my phone, which was in my hands. "Boy, ain't nobody gotta lie to you. I told you they started renovating just months ago. It's almost done. They told me it's livable, but with Harmony's allergies, I don't want to chance the dust and shit."

The lies just rolled off my tongue so effortlessly, but I knew I couldn't keep this up long, especially with me carrying this man's child. He had to learn the truth sooner than later.

"Aw, yeah, speaking of Harmony, I got something for her," he said, standing up, pulling a folded piece of paper from his back pocket.

"What's this?" I asked as he slid the paper across the table.

JA motioned with his head for me to open it and see for myself, and that was exactly what I did.

"Oh my God, JA, you did not!" I squirmed excitedly in my seat.

JA had gotten Harmony front row tickets to Future's concert after I had told him that it was sold out.

"How did you?" I asked curiously.

"You know I'm that nigga, babbbyyyy" he smirked, taking a sip of his Pepsi.

"No, seriously, how?" I asked again.

"Damn! Why, Princess? Whhhyyyyy!!!" he playfully yelled.

I couldn't help but laugh. This man had people around us, staring at his goofy ass.

"But nah, me and Future got the same jeweler, and I did business with him a few times. I sent him a text and his manager emailed me these this morning," he finally admitted.

"Thanks so much, baby. Harmony gon' go crazy!" I said, leaning forward in my seat, giving him a kiss.

"You're welcome. Anything for my baby girl. My invisible baby girl."

I knew it had to be bothering JA that I'd never allowed him to meet Harmony although he'd never said it. There were a lot of things I had to fix and come clean about, sooner than later, I just hoped he could handle my secret lifestyle.

JA

I rambled through the cabinet in my bathroom, looking for some type of medicine. At this point, I didn't care what type it was, I just needed something to make this cold go away. It was early September, and still fairly hot outside, but here I was, wrapped up in a cover, feeling like I was on my deathbed. I was the type of nigga who got sick once every blue moon, but when I did get hit with a virus, the shit fucked me up good.

"Man, this some bullshit!" I yelled, slamming the glass door and heading back to my bedroom.

Once inside, I grabbed the remote control off the floor, placed the covers on top of me and turned on *Martin*. I thought about calling Princess and bugging her, but tonight was the Future concert, and I didn't want to ruin it for her or Harmony, so I just manned up and dealt with it.

After watching about three episodes on the Firestick, I grabbed my phone to look at the time. It was fifteen minutes after eleven, and I was hungrier than a motherfucker. I sat there for a minute, thinking of places that delivered this late, but my mind drew a blank. Just as I was about to download the "UberEats" app, my phone began to ring. I looked at a picture of Princess on my screen and answered.

"Hello."

"Hey, baby! You sound bad. Are you OK?" she asked.

"Yeah, I'm straight. I was just about to order something to eat."

"What you about to order?" she questioned.

"I don't know yet, baby. Something. How was the concert?"

Princess laughed before continuing, "Babbbbyyyy, we were so turnt up. Harmony still turnt. Our seats were so damn close, it felt like we were on the stage. Future killed it," she cooed.

"Well, I'm glad y'all enjoyed y'all selves," I said, followed by a hard cough.

"Ugh, maybe you need to go to the ER," she encouraged.

"Nah… I'm good." I coughed again.

"Aye, baby, let me call you right back," Princess said, ending the call abruptly.

I decided not to order anything to eat. I was sleepy and figured I'd be knocked out by the time it got here anyway. I watched one last episode of *Martin*, my favorite one when Biggie Smalls came to Detroit looking for backup singers. Once that episode ended, I got up to get a bottle of water. When I made it downstairs to the kitchen, my doorbell rang. Without hesitation, I went to answer it. I figured it was Smoke coming through because he had gotten into it with his baby momma again, but to my surprise, when I opened the door, Princess and Harmony were standing there with a bag from Walgreens and White Castles.

"Somebody called for a doctor?" Harmony asked, handing me her bag that was filled with cough drops, Nyquil, and orange juice.

"Awwww, thanks, shorty," I replied, grabbing my medicine and moving to the side to allow them entrance.

Harmony was more beautiful than the pictures Princess had shown me. She looked like her twin: slanted, brown eyes, sandy brown hair and a few freckles planted across her face.

"Here, I got you two double cheeseburgers...extra pickles, and a six-piece chicken rings," Princess said, placing the greasy bag on the kitchen counter.

"Thanks, baby. I'm finna fuck this up... Oh shit... Damn, my bad, Harmony." I quickly apologized for cursing.

"It's cool, JA. My momma mouth wayyyyy nastier than that," she commented, causing all of us to laugh.

"Girl, shut up. I guess I should formally introduce y'all. JA, this is the love of my life, Harmony, and Harmony, this is JA."

"Hey, Harmony, I've heard a lot about you," I exclaimed, giving her a playful handshake.

"Nice to FINALLY meet you, JA," Harmony replied, cutting her eyes at Princess.

After everyone got acquainted, we began to eat our food. Harmony walked over to the kitchen counter near Princess, grabbing an onion ring out of the bag, throwing it in her mouth. She then went over and whispered something in Princess' ear that caused her to laugh loudly.

"Girrrrrllll, hush," Princess said, playfully pushing her.

"What happened?" I questioned.

"Nooooo, mommy... You bet' not... Pleassseeeee!!" Harmony squirmed, trying to place her hand over Princess' mouth, attempting to silence her.

"Girl, movvveeee. This damn child of mine gon' whisper in my ear and say, 'Ma, he's soooo handsome'," Princess teased.

I looked over at Harmony, who turned red from embarrassment as she buried her face in her hands.

"It's cool, Harmony, but Princess, you petty as hell for tricking on her."

"Thanks, JA, my momma doesn't understand," Harmony said shyly.

"It's cool. You got a PS4 at the crib?" I asked, changing the subject.

"Yeah, I play it all the time," she replied.

"Aw, straight up! What's your favorite game?"

"Ummmmm, *Call of Duty*," she replied.

"Damn, that's my shit. Me and my homies be playing together. I bet I could kick yo' ass like I do them," I boasted.

"Put yo' money where yo' mouth is and let's do this." She smiled from ear to ear.

"Say no more, follow me."

Harmony and I headed to the game room located in the basement of my house. I was a game head growing up, so it was only right that I had the games that I had grown up on. I owned the original *Mrs. Pac-Man*, the arcade version, a pool table, darts, the original Nintendo, PS4 and Xbox One. The crazy thing is, I was barely home to play, but on days like today, when I was sick or when the weather was fucking up in the winter, I took advantage of it.

I hooked everything up, and Harmony and I got right down to business. We were so into the game and each other's company, we hadn't even noticed that Princess had never come down to join us. I glanced over at the clock on the wall, and it was almost two a.m. I didn't have to be a parent to know that it was passed a ten-year-old's bedtime, so I wrapped things up.

"A'ight, you beat my ass, Harmony. Let's go see what Mommy up to," I announced after letting her win a few times.

"Cool!" she replied, hopping up and heading up the stairs.

I had to admit that Harmony was one cool-ass kid. While playing the game, she told me about school, friends and basically everything going on in the average kid's life. Meeting her made me feel some type of way. I was glad that Princess felt like we were at a point in our relationship where she trusted me being around her kid.

When we entered the living room, Princess was knocked out cold with the remote still in her hand. I looked over at Harmony, whose eyes locked with mine at the same time.

"Aye, go in the refrigerator and grab the chocolate syrup," I whispered to her.

An evil grin spread across her face before she took off in the direction of the kitchen. She returned with the chocolate syrup in hand, ready for the next instructions.

"A'ight, go ahead," I said, shoving her towards Princess.

"Now, JA, if she whoops me, I'ma be mad at you," Harmony protested.

"Man, gon' and stop being a punk," I encouraged her.

"I ain't no punk, watch this," Harmony said, tip-toeing over to the couch.

She paused briefly as Princess slightly shifted in her sleep, she then unlatched the top and turned the bottle upside down, right over Princess' head, squeezing for dear life. The chocolate oozed out of the brand-new bottle and landed right on top of her forehead.

"WHAT THE FUCK!" Princess jumped up, startled.

Unable to speak, both Harmony and I bent over, laughing uncontrollably.

"I'm finna fuck y'all up!" she yelled, wiping her face.

"RUN, HARMONY!" I screamed as Harmony took off up the stairs with Princess in tow.

I spent the next hour, breaking Harmony and Princess up. Before any of us knew it, it was damn near three in the morning. I offered my guest room to them, but Princess declined, but I couldn't blame her. I was cool with her allowing me to be a part of her daughter's life.

A Secret Hood Love Affair

PRINCESS

"Princess, look at youuuuuuu! Your once flat stomach is starting to poke out now," Courtney drilled me.

"I know. I know. I know. But I need you to focus on the task at hand," I replied, referring to the pieces of fabric in front of us.

"The task you are dealing with right now is bigger than some fuckin' Halloween costumes," she snapped.

"OK, what, Courtney? WHAT?" I snapped back, turning to her, giving her my full attention.

"Look at you, you're living a lie—"

"HOW?" I cut her off.

"What the fuck you mean how? You are almost four months pregnant by a man who doesn't even know he has a child on the way. Then, on top of that, you've fallen in love with him. He loves your dirty drawers and don't know your true lifestyle. I mean, how long are you going to keep all this from him?"

I took a deep breath and rolled my eyes. I felt like I was getting scolded by my mom while sitting in the principal's office. I couldn't be upset with Courtney because she was speaking the truth, especially about the falling in love part. I was crazy about JA, and he was crazy about both myself and Harmony. He had become a major factor in her life these last two months. I hated that I had to train her on what not to say around JA. Harmony understood for the most part about our family being a big deal, but not to the extent of being a drug cartel.

"You know what, cousin, you are right, and I'm going to tell JA tomorrow, after the party at the club. I don't need to be thinking about the shit at our Halloween party tonight," I agreed.

"Whatever, let's find this wig so your costume can be complete," she said, slightly dismissing me.

After leaving the store with Courtney, I headed to pick up Harmony from school. After waiting in the pickup lane, which seemed like forever, she finally sashayed her ass out of the building, and into my truck.

"Hey, baby, how was school?" I asked.

"Hey, Ma, it was OK," she replied dryly.

"What's wrong?"

"Nothing," she responded before putting her headphones in her ears.

I was going to investigate more, but I had to realize that I was the mother of an almost teenager, and there were going to be some things I had to allow her to come to me about, instead of hammering her about it.

fter riding in silence for about ten minutes, I removed one of the headphones from her ear. "Wanna go get frozen yogurt?" I asked.

"Which place are we going to?"

"The one downtown, why?"

"The one by JA's bar?"

"Yes, Harmony, why?" I questioned again.

"Nothing, I'll text him," she said, pulling her phone from her pocket.

I shook my head and continued to Forever Frozen Yogurt on Ohio Street. Once I pulled in the parking lot, I noticed JA's car pulling in directly behind me.

"What he doing here?" I wondered.

"I texted him and asked if he wanted to join us," she explained.

"Damn, Harmony, how you know this wasn't a mommy and daughter thing?"

"Ma, you have me all the time. Stop being selfish," she replied, unbuckling her seatbelt and getting out the car.

I followed close behind and watched her run up to JA, doing this "secret" handshake they had created.

"What's up, baby?" he said, greeting me with a kiss.

"Hey, babe," I said.

I got in between them and grabbed their hands as we made our way inside the store.

The place was packed, so we ordered our treats and headed back out. On the way to the car, Harmony pulled me to the side and asked if she could talk to JA alone for a second. Instantly, my antennas went up, but I trusted their bond, so I didn't object.

"Go ahead, but don't be long. You know my party tonight," I warned her.

"OK, mommy, I'll be right back," she replied, skipping over to his car.

I scrolled on Facebook, accepting and rejecting friend requests while I waited for Harmony to come back to the car. She popped back up about five minutes later with a smile on her face.

"What was that about?" I inquired, cranking up the car.

"Nothing, Ma. I didn't say anything I wasn't supposed to say," she confirmed, and I trusted her enough not to question her any further.

***

The line to get into Daddy's Girl was wrapped around the corner. Everyone in their lavish costumes looked amazing. Halloween was my favorite holiday, and JA and I had done it big our first one together. We pulled up and stepped out an old-school Cadillac, looking like the real Ike and Tina. I wore a gold, ripped-up spandex dress with black, six-inch heels. The honey brown wig, which was cut into layers, fit my face perfectly, accompanied by fire red MAC lipstick and a face full of makeup.

Ike, I mean, JA, wore a pair of bell bottoms and a flowered buttoned-up shirt with the top three buttons undone. A black fro wig and a pair of Timbs that I had tried to talk him out of wearing, but he refused to be caught in platform heels, even on Halloween.

When we stepped out onto the red carpet, all eyes landed on us as most people pulled out their phones to take pictures. As soon as we walked in, the DJ started playing the scene from *What's Love Got To Do With It* when they fought in the limo on the huge projector over the stage.

"Aye, bae, this bitch cracking!" JA yelled over the music.

"Hell yeah. I didn't expect the turnout to be this big, especially since none of my girls was actually stripping tonight," I shouted back.

"I told you it would be a good idea," he bragged.

"Shut up, let's get a drink," I replied, pulling him towards the bar with me.

After we ordered our drinks, we chilled and listened to the music. It made me think back to the first time we met and bonded in the club. Who would have thought, five months later, we would be the "IT" couple, and I would be pregnant by him?

"Look at these fools," I said, pointing to the dance floor as Courtney and Mocha made it over to us.

They looked so cute in their costumes. Courtney was dressed as Cleo from *Set It Off*, and Mocha wore her hair in a super short blonde cut, exactly like Queen Latifah's girlfriend character in the movie. I suggested they go as Ellen DeGeneres and her wife, Portia de Rossi, but I was glad they hadn't listened to me because they were killing this look.

"Hey, Anna Mae. What's up, Ike?" Courtney spoke.

"Hey, girl," I spoke back while JA's cool ass gave a cool-ass nod.

"Y'all, this bitch live tonight!" Mocha yelled, looking around the packed club.

"Ain't it, man," Courtney co-signed.

The three of them took back to back shots. I lied and said my stomach was cramping, so I settled for juice. About thirty minutes later, Smoke and his baby momma joined us. Brittany was a cute, petite, chocolate girl with a short cut, and she put me in the mind of Kelly Rowland back in her younger Destiny's Child days. This was my first time meeting her, and I must say, I was pleasantly surprised. JA teased Smoke all the time about their issues, so I thought she'd be ratchet, but she wasn't, which was a good thing.

While standing there, I started to feel a little woozy. I knew I had to throw up, but now was not the time or place. Courtney must have noticed the look on my face because she asked everyone to step outside with her so she could smoke. I looked over at my favorite cousin and smiled, and she returned the expression with a wink.

While outside, the crisp, fall air crept up my dress, and it felt wonderful. Fresh air was exactly what I needed because I felt better immediately. I pulled out my phone to shoot Harmony a goodnight text when I heard a female's voice.

"Bitch, I hope you ain't think it was over."

I looked up the street and recognized the person; it was the same bitch I had beat up at JA's house a few months back, Tika. I looked over at JA, who looked like he was ready to go off. Smoke stood there, shaking his head, Courtney and Brittany both looked confused, while Mocha knew what was up and started stepping out of her heels. I followed her lead and did the same. I was tired of this bitch, and you'd think she would have had enough from the last ass whooping I had given her.

"Tika, yo' ass better gone," JA said, stepping into her path.

"Move, JA!" she demanded, trying to walk past him.

"Who the fuck is this bitch?" Courtney asked, pointing her finger in Tika's face.

"This the li'l hoe I whooped back at JA's crib," I filled her in.

"Naw, Princess, you beat the brakes off that bitch," Smoke added.

"Bitch, you caught me off guard. Square up now," she challenged.

I guess the bitch was brave because of the two other bitches standing behind her, but I was pretty sure they didn't know what they were getting themselves into.

"What up?" I said, stepping around JA just enough to get a clear shot of her face.

"Dammmmmnnnnnn!" Smoke yelled out once my fist contacted with Tika's face.

Before she could get to me, Mocha and Brittany were beating her and her friend's ass, while Courtney held me back.

"LET ME THE FUCK GOOOOO!!" I yelled, trying my best to get away.

"No, bitch, you pregnant. You not finna be out here fighting!" Courtney yelled back.

It was like all background noise stopped when she said those magic words, and silence fell upon everyone's ears.

"She what?" JA turned around and asked.

I heard everything that Courtney said and JA's reaction to the news, but I was too pissed at this point to react. I hated being tried, and Tika had tried me too many times. Three strikes and you're out. I was mad at myself for being in this costume and not having my pistol on me. I promised her the last time I saw her that any further meetings would result in her losing her life. I had no problem popping this bitch and having my dad and uncle handle whatever happened afterwards.

"EVERYBODY CALM THE FUCK DOWN!" JA yelled, his voice seeming to quiet the confrontation immediately.

Along with Smoke and Courtney's help, JA was able to break everybody up and separate the two groups.

"I'm sick of this bitch snaking me," Tika cried out from behind Smoke.

"Ohhhh, you gotta be quicker than that," I laughed. "But you better be glad that's all I did," I continued.

"I swear to God, bitch, I'm killing you!" Tika screamed, jumping up and down.

"Man, let's go, we need to talk," JA said, pulling me away from the crowd and back towards the club.

I hesitantly followed him in the direction he was pulling me in. I knew where this was headed, and to be honest, I wanted no parts of it.

JA

"It's taking everything in me not to bug up on yo' ass, Princess," I growled as soon as her office doors closed.

"JA, I'm sorry, but—"

"BUT WHAT?" I cut her off.

"I can't believe you would keep some shit like this from me," I continued.

"I didn't know how you would react," she replied in her defense.

"React? Shorty, I love the fuck outta you. How you think I'd react?"

I could tell I had caught Princess off guard with my last comment. I had even caught myself off guard. There was no secret that I liked Princess, cared deeply about her, but neither one of us had ever uttered the L-word before.

"It's just that since it happened the very first time we had sex, I was hesitant," she finally replied.

"The first time. You serious?" I questioned.

"Dead ass," she stated before taking a seat on her desk.

I stood there and thought back to the very first time we fucked in California. We'd never used protection, but I guess pregnancy never crossed my mind. I glanced down at her stomach, and I could shoot myself in the leg. How the fuck hadn't I noticed her belly poking out like it was?

"Have you been to the doctor?" I questioned.

"Yeah, I go back next week to see what I'm having."

"PRINCESS... EXACTLY HOW FAR ALONG ARE YOU?" I raised my voice.

Princess looked down at her feet before mumbling, "Almost five months."

This night was getter crazier and crazier. First, my ex-bitch popped up at my girl's club, acting a fool, then I find out my girl damn near in labor. This shit was too much for a nigga like me.

"I'm sorry, JA. I know I'm wrong, but I didn't know how to tell you," she looked up and said with tears in her eyes.

"Aye, come here, man," I replied, taking a few steps forward, grabbing her by both arms and pulling her close to me.

"You don't ever have to be scared to tell me shit. I fucks with you, Princess, and to be honest, I fucks with you even harder now because you got my shorty in there," I explained, rubbing her hard belly.

Princess looked up at me while tears fell down her cheeks. This was my first time seeing her get emotional like this. I removed my hand from her stomach and wiped the tears from her eyes.

"Look, no more secrets, a'ight?" I said, lifting her chin, forcing her to look me in the eyes.

"No more secrets... I love you, JA," she replied, kissing me on the lips.

"I love you, too."

Princess and I engaged in a long kiss until she pulled away and stepped back. I could tell by the new found look on her face that something was bugging her.

"What?" I blurted.

Princess placed both of her hands on her hips before replying. "Why this Tika bitch keep popping up?"

I looked at her and laughed a little before shaking my head. "I have no idea. I don't fuck with her, ain't trying to fuck with her."

"Well, she seems to think differently, and the fact that the bitch threatened me is not sitting right with me."

"Look, I'ma handle her, you handle our child, and we all gon' be good," I assured her.

"A'ight, cuz it ain't shit to get her ass murked," Princess stated before heading out of the office.

"Murked? Who the fuck do you belong to? A mob boss," I laughed.

"You getting warmer," she replied, chuckling.

The rest of the night, we partied in VIP and got fucked up. While I was knocking back shots, it dawned on me that every time liquor was involved these past few months, Princess never engaged. She always had an excuse. I still couldn't believe pregnancy was the reason. I let Smoke know that I was about to be a dad and this nigga brought the bar out. Despite all the drama, this had actually turned out to be a good night.

The next morning, I woke up to an empty bed. I sat up and looked around the room, but there was no sign of Princess. I was drunk this morning when we made it in but not to the point where I was tweaking,. I knew she had spent the night at my crib. I got up and headed downstairs where I found Princess on my couch with a lemon in one hand and the jar of olives in the other hand.

"Shorty!" I said, stopping halfway down the stairs.

"What?" she asked with a mouth full of olives.

I laughed to myself before joining her on the couch. I took a seat directly next to her, lifted her legs and placed them on my lap.

"I can't believe you been hiding this from me. I can't believe I never caught on," I admitted, glancing over at her.

"Awwwww, I apologize, but just know it wasn't easy. I used to pray to God whenever I was around you that I didn't throw up or nothing," she confessed.

I had every reason to be upset with Princess, but my anger was overruled by the fact that I was about to be a father. I couldn't wait to tell my family. Well, technically, all I had to do was tell my OG, and the whole family would know in a matter of minutes.

"So, other than Courtney and Mocha, who else knows you popped?" I questioned.

Princess leaned forward and set the empty jar of olives on the floor before speaking. "Just them two. Well, the three of y'all, including you."

"That's crazy. So, when is your next appointment? When will we figure out what we having? Have you been taking vitamins? Princess, don't do shit to fuck up my child's brain," I warned her.

Princess must have thought I was joking by the way she started laughing, but I was dead ass serious. Once she noticed the stern look on my face, she became quiet.

"I just told you all this last night, but my next appointment is next Thursday. If this baby cooperates, we should know what we are having then, and I take all the prescriptions they prescribed to me and then some. Chill, baby daddy, I got this," she said, standing.

"Aye, Princess," I said, reaching out, grabbing her by the arm before she made it too far.

She stopped in her stride and turned around, looking at me.

"What's up?" she asked.

I looked her in the eyes before saying, "I love you."

A warm smile invaded her face. "I love you, too."

Princess bent down and placed a soft kiss on my lips before heading towards the kitchen.

"Princess!" I called out to her again, grabbing that same arm.

"What, JA?" she chuckled.

"Look, I heard that pregnant pussy is bomb. Let me see if they lying or not!" I stated.

Princess smacked her lips before placing her hands on her hips.

"Boy, you been fucking pregnant pussy all this time, you just didn't know it."

"Exactly, that's my point. That shit don't count," I informed her.

Princess laughed again before walking into the kitchen and returning to the living room seconds later. She stood in front of me, parting my legs with her legs, getting in between them. She licked her lips seductively, and even without a dab of makeup on, and her long hair in two braids, she was still the baddest woman on the planet. I sat back and admired her beauty. I was a lucky man, and she had a nigga thinking about settling down for good.

Princess began to pull the peach lace panties she was wearing down, slowly stepping out of them and exposing her freshly waxed vagina. She then hovered over me, taking her right hand, going inside my Nike basketball shorts, pulling out my already hard dick. Princess smiled before straddling me, easing her way down all ten inches like a pro. I knew she was in pain even though she tried to mask it, but she got an A for effort. I grabbed her by the waist, giving her guidance as her juices flooded my manhood.

"Gotttt dammmmmnnnnn, Princess!" I said, letting out a loud moan.

At this point, I didn't give a fuck about sounding like a little bitch. She rode the shit out of my dick. I removed my hands from her small waist and placed them on her fat ass, assisting her as she bounced up and down.

"Now, what about pregnant pussy?" she moaned softly.

It took me a while to reply, I was lost in the sauce. "Pregnant pussy about to get yo' ass pregnant again… I'm about to cummmmm!"

As soon as those words were released from my lips, my nut released inside of Princess. I could tell she was almost at her peak as well by the way she sped up.

"Come on, baby," I said, egging her on. I wasn't sure how much more I was going to be able to take myself.

"Fuuuucccckkkkkk, JA, I'm cumming!" she screamed before collapsing on my chest.

Now, don't get me wrong, I loved Princess to death, but she had to get her ass off my soft dick. She must have read my mind because she eased her way up, but not before I got one last smack on that ass. I watched her ass jiggle and instantly got hard. I called out to her as she walked up the stairs. "Aye, bae, I think pregnant pussy wack. Come here so I can try again."

Princess laughed before turning around and sticking up her middle finger, disappearing into the bedroom.

PRINCESS

"Mommy, where are we going?" Harmony asked from the passenger seat of my Jeep Cherokee.

I looked over at my baby and smiled. "It's a surprise, and you'll see in a few minutes. We almost there," I informed her.

Harmony gave me the side-eye before crossing her arms and looking out the window. She was so damn impatient, but I knew she didn't get that from anyone but myself. About ten minutes later, I turned into the parking lot of Mile Square Clinic, found a parking spot a few feet away, parked, and killed the engine. I reached into the back seat for my Chanel purse when I noticed a confused look on my child's face.

"Mommy, are you serious? This the surprise? I just seen Dr. Wallace. What type of surprise is this?" she quizzed.

"Harmony, shut up, get out, and watch that car right there," I fussed before jumping out myself.

When I got out, I reached in my purse for my phone, shooting JA a text message.

Me: WYA?

JA: I'll be there in ten minutes, I had to take care of some business.

Me: Yup.

JA: Princess don't start that shit.

Instead of replying, I tossed my phone back in my Chanel bag and proceeded into the clinic. I checked in at the front desk before joining Harmony in the waiting area.

"So, Ma, why are we here again?" she asked.

I was becoming annoyed by the second. This child and her twenty-one questions and JA's ass never being on time for shit was pissing me off. I knew my horrible attitude had something to do with these pregnancy hormones, so that was why I tried my best to control my mouth.

"I have a doctor's appointment, baby," I finally replied.

Harmony said, "Aw, OK," and continued to watch YouTube videos on her phone. After waiting for what seemed like an hour, JA finally walked in wearing a gray Nike jogging suit and a fresh pair of white Ones. I laughed out loud as the other pregnant bitches and their friends' heads turned and stared at him. He spotted me over in the corner and walked over wearing that smile that I loved so much.

"What's up, baby?"

Harmony's head popped up, along with her body. "Jaaaaaaaaaa!" She squirmed, giving him a hug.

"What you watching?" he asked, snatching her phone out of her hands.

JA looked at whatever was playing on Harmony's phone for a few seconds before handing it back to her.

"Sup, baby!" I finally greeted him once he took a seat in the available chair next to me.

"Shit, I had to handle some business," he replied.

"Everything straight?" I asked.

"Yup!"

JA and I made small talk until my name was called. We then made our way to the back, with Harmony in tow.

"OK, Ms. Taylor, undress from the waist up. Here is a sheet to cover up with, and someone will be in to see you in a few minutes," the nice medical assistant instructed before leaving out.

I began to take off the Gucci blouse I was wearing when I noticed the confused look on Harmony's face. JA must have noticed too because he started laughing.

"Baby girl, you good?" he asked her.

"I'm lost. Mommy, what you doing, and why yo' stomach look like that? Oh my God!" she said, placing her hands over her mouth.

JA and I both burst out in laughter. Harmony was so extra and dramatic.

"Mommy, are you pregnant?" she asked, finally calming down a little.

"Yeah, baby, that's the surprise!" I replied, grinning.

"I cannot believe this. I cannot believe this," she repeated as she paced in a small circle.

"Girl, sit down!" I yelled, pulling her by the arm.

"I'm just so happy, y'all! I was so sick and tired of being the only child, and Ma, can I be honest about something?" she asked, looking back and forth between JA and myself.

"Yeah, baby, go ahead," I encouraged her.

"I was just telling my friend Kierra that you were getting fat. I didn't want to tell you because I didn't want to hurt your feelings," she rambled on.

Harmony kept the rant going until the ultrasound tech came in and started the procedure. Both her and JA's eyes were glued to the monitor as if they knew what they were looking at.

"OK, the babies are looking good," the technician confirmed.

"Wait. Wait. Wait. The who?" I asked, sitting up the best way I could so I could get a better view of what she was looking at.

"The babies. See, look here," she replied, pointing to the screen.

"Here's the sack, and here's baby A and baby B. They share the same sack, therefore, they are identical," she continued.

"GET THE FUCK OUTTA HERE!" JA jumped up and yelled.

"Yes, daddy, you will be the proud father of identical boys. See!" The technician punched something on the keyboard, and two arrows appeared, pointing at their little penises.

The look on JA's face made me want to cry. I had never seen him so happy, nor had I ever thought he would be this excited. He always told me how happy he was that I was carrying his child, but to actually see his reaction brought tears to my eyes.

The technician printed out some copies of the results for us before we left. JA stared at the pictures until we made it to the parking lot.

"So, Harmony, how do you feel about me and JA having a baby?" I questioned my ten-year-old.

"I'm happy, y'all. Slightly overwhelmed, though. I only wanted one brother, and now I'm about to have two. This is too much for my little heart," she replied, placing her right hand over her heart.

The three of us started laughing. "You sure she ain't been here before?" JA asked.

"She sure do act like it, right!" I agreed with him.

JA walked Harmony and I to my car and Harmony jumped right in while I stood out there with him.

"Aye, follow me," he instructed.

"Follow you where?" I quizzed.

"To my OG's crib. I gotta tell her about the boys, and I want you to be there, too."

"A'ight, let me drop Harmony off first," I told him.

"For what? She's coming, too. Try to keep up in that little-ass Jeep," was all he said before kissing me and walking off to his Maserati.

I stuck up my middle finger before hopping inside, cranking the car up and peeling off.

"Ma, where we going now?" Harmony asked.

"To JA's mother's house," I replied, weaving through traffic, secretly trying to beat him there.

"Aw... And speaking of mothers, do MaMa and PaPa know about the babies?" she asked.

I quickly turned my head and looked at her. I tried to push the lies about my life and family to the back of my mind, but there was always Courtney, and now Harmony, reminding me. I planned on telling JA the truth tonight, I just hoped it didn't turn him off or even scare him off.

"Naw, baby, I haven't told them yet, and I need you to keep your mouth shut, too. Do you understand me?" I asked sternly.

"Yeah, Ma, but I don't get why we are keeping all these secrets. First, from JA, and now MaMa and PaPa."

"It's so complicated, baby. You'll understand when you get older. Until then, just don't say anything, OK?"

"OK!"

JA

I couldn't stop thinking about the twins. I prayed that I had a son, but to be blessed with two was crazy. I couldn't wait to tell my OG. All she talked about was grandkids, and she knew Sky wasn't giving her any anytime soon, and to be perfectly honest, I didn't think I was either. I watched Princess through my rearview mirror, trying to keep up with me on the expressway. I purposely dipped in and out of traffic just to throw her off, but she was hanging in there. About ten minutes later, I pulled up to my mother's driveway with Princess right behind me. I cut the car off and hopped out and waited for Princess and Harmony to wrap up whatever conversation they were having, and the three of us went up the stairs to my mother's door.

"I understand you got a key and all, but don't you think you should knock?" Princess stated.

I turned around and looked at her before replying, "Knock for what?"

"What if she got a man in there and we bussing in, fuckin' up they groove," she replied.

"Well, buddy won't be nutting today," was my response before turning the key and letting myself in.

My mom's house always smelled like lemon Pine-Sol. Ever since I was younger, she swore on a bible that that was the best shit ever. I even brought over some new cleaning supplies for her to try out, but she just tossed that shit to the back of the closet and proceeded with the lemon fresh scent Pine-Sol bullshit.

"Aye, yo, Maaaaa!" I yelled out from the living room.

Harmony giggled while Princess punched me in the arm. Moments later, my mother appeared from upstairs wearing a Bebe jogging suit, socks, and a scarf on her head.

"Boy, why the fuck are you hollering in my house like that? Oh, I'm sorry. I didn't know you had someone with you," she continued once she noticed Princess and Harmony standing there.

"It's cool, Janice. I would have cursed him out too had he come in my house hollering like that," Princess added.

My mother laughed before giving Princess a hug. In the middle of their embrace, she pulled back and stared at her, placing her hand on her stomach.

"Why yo' stomach so hard?" she asked with a puzzled look on her face.

I looked at Princess, who just smiled. My mother then looked over at me for confirmation, but I just shrugged.

"Somebody here better tell me something," my mother stated, placing her hands on her hips.

"Don't feel bad, they didn't tell me either," Harmony said out of nowhere.

Everyone laughed, while my mom directed her attention to Harmony.

"And who is this beautiful little lady here?" my mom asked.

"My name is Harmony. I'm her daughter," Harmony answered, pointing to Princess.

"Oh my God, Harmony, you are so pretty," my mom complimented her.

"Thank you!" Harmony replied, blushing.

"OK, now back to the matter at hand. Harmony, what are they keeping from us?" My mother picked up right where she left off.

Harmony looked at me first, then over at Princess for confirmation. Princess gave a slight head nod, and Harmony took that opportunity and ran with it.

"OK, Miss JA's Mom, I had been saying to my friend at school, her name is Kierra, that my mommy was getting fat, but I didn't want to tell my mommy that because I love her, and I would never want to hurt her feelings. So, today, she tells me that we are going out for a surprise, and I was so mad when we pulled up to the doctor's office because I had just been to Dr. Wallace not even a month ago. Fast forward, we in the room and my mommy starts taking off her clothes, and I'm wondering why, then she tells me she's pregnant. I was sooooo happy, Ms. JA's Mom because I never have nobody to play with. I keep telling my cousin Courtney to have a baby so me and her baby can be close like her and my mom but she keeps saying that that will never happen," Harmony paused.

"Ohhhhh, so, Harmony, we are having a baby. Is that right?" my mom chimed in, looking at both me and Princess, smiling.

"Yep! But guess what, we not only having one baby, we have two. The lady told my mommy and JA that we were having twins, twin boys, but I don't know how I feel about that. I can deal with one brother, but two? I know that's gon' drive me crazy," Harmony said, continuing her rant.

"Wait, twins! Get the fuck outta here!" my mother yelled.

"That's the same way I reacted, Ma," I said, filling her in.

My mother and Princess made plans for the baby shower, and they even discussed names. My mother FaceTimed Sky, who was in Atlanta at school, and told her the news. Sky was more excited than any of us. She begged me to fly her home for the weekend just so she could go baby shopping.

"I know all three of my grandbabies are hungry," my mom stated, referring to the twins and Harmony.

"We are starving," Harmony spoke up before Princess could.

"See, I knew it. I'll whip up something for dinner," my mother announced, standing.

"No, that won't be necessary. As a matter of fact, tonight is family dinner night. Once a week, my family has dinner, and it's forbidden for anyone to miss it," Princess informed her.

"Aw, yeah, I forgot about that," my mom replied, sitting back down.

Princess wore the same look of confusion on her face as I did. "What you mean, you forgot?" I questioned my mom.

"Aw, boy, nothing. I was thinking about something else," she replied, dismissing it.

"So, we about to head out. Baby, I want to invite you over tonight. Can you make it?" Princess asked, catching me off guard.

"Yeah, pleasssseeee come, JA!" Harmony whined, poking out her bottom lip.

Shit was moving too fast. First, I found out that I was about to have twins, then Princess wanted to invite me to dinner with her bourgeois-ass family. I mean, Princess, Courtney and Harmony weren't bourgeois, but I could only imagine how a doctor and lawyer would react when their pregnant daughter brought her boyfriend, who was the drug connect and plug for the whole Midwest, home to dinner. I thought about backing out of it, but I didn't want to disappoint her or Harmony, so I agreed. Shit had to happen sooner or later, so might as well get it out the way.

"A'ight, let me use the bathroom, and we can bounce."

I went down the hall to relieve myself. Once I was done, I washed my hands and headed back towards the living room when my phone rang. I pulled it out my pocket and answered the call.

"Yo!"

"I got a proposition for you," Andre, one of the workers who worked alongside the Taylor twins said from the other end of the phone.

"What up? I'm listening," I replied, leaning against the wall in the hallway.

Andre ran me a script, and it was more than a proposition; it was the business venture I'd been waiting for. He told me that he needed to holler at me right now, and although I had promised Princess I would come over to her crib, unfortunately, that would have to wait. Andre sent me a text with the address to where I was meeting him, and I told him I was on my way before joining the ladies in the living room.

"Boy, did you spray?" my mother asked as soon as I entered.

"Hell nah, you gon' enjoy my shit!" I replied jokingly.

"A'ight, Ma, we finna head out," I stated, walking towards the door.

"OK. Y'all be safe and have fun. Remember things happen for a reason. It's only so long you can hide the truth," she stated before I began to close the door.

"What the fuck is that supposed to mean, Ma?" I asked.

"You'll see," was all she said before I closed the front door.

PRINCESS

"Really, JA?"

"My bad, baby. I swear I'll make it up to you, but I gotta handle this business. Look, I'll swing by after I'm done. I'll make sure it's not too late so I can still meet your people," he replied, trying his hardest to convince me.

I couldn't lie, I was extremely disappointed. I had finally built enough courage to invite him to meet my family, and now he wasn't able to make it. I was a strong believer in the saying, "Everything happens for a reason," therefore, I just let it be. There was always next time.

"Look, after I handle the business at the car dealership, I'm going to swing by the bar, and I'll call you. Again, baby, I'm so sorry," he apologized again.

I rolled my eyes before grabbing Harmony's hand, leading her to the car. Regardless of how I had just tried to convince myself not to be mad, I was pissed. Not only was I pissed, but I was also tired of lying about who my family really was. I was tired of lying, saying that my house was still being worked on. We had been together five months, and he had never even been to my crib. I was tired of a lot of shit.

The entire ride back to the estate was quiet, and that was only because Harmony had fallen asleep before we even hit the expressway. Outside of JA not being able to join us for dinner, the day was awesome. I loved JA's family's reaction to the news of the pregnancy, I just hoped my family reacted the same way. I had been purposely avoiding them the best way I could for the last month or so. When I was around them, I made sure I wore loose fitting clothes. My daddy and uncle had been extra busy lately, in and out of the country, so I didn't have to avoid them much.

It took me about an hour to get home; the traffic to Olympia Fields was ridiculous. As soon as I made it past the security gates, I went straight to my parents' house. Dinner was set to start in thirty minutes, so I figured I'd just lay down in my old room until everything was finalized. I walked past the two armed, big-ass guardsmen at the front door and entered the mansion. The smell of greens, ham, sweet potatoes and cornbread made me smile as well as caused the boys to move inside my stomach. It was kind of weird to have this as dinner so close to Thanksgiving, but the way my hunger was set up, I was not the one to complain.

"Dadddddyyyyyy!!!" I screamed out as soon as I spotted him in his office when I turned the corner.

Both Harmony and I ran at top speed, trying to beat each other. I lightly pushed her, which caused her to fall onto the leather couch next to his desk.

"Really, Mommy? You cheated," she whined, standing up.

"So what, I missed my daddy," I teased.

"Princess, you wrong for that. Come here PaPa baby, there's room in these arms for you, too," my daddy stated, grabbing Harmony with his free hand, pulling her into our three-way hug.

"So, how was Cuba?" I asked, taking a seat on the couch.

"It's beautiful, baby. Too bad it's always business and never pleasure. What's been going on with you?" he asked, grabbing a metal case out of his desk drawer and pulling out a fat cigar.

"Everything been cool. Daddy's Girls and Taylor Made are both doing great. I think I need a vacation," I assured him.

"Yeah, I was talking to your mother about planning a family vacation. We haven't had one since last year. As soon as I'm done finalizing this deal, we gon' take flight."

I laughed at my father's choice of words. *Take flight*. He always tried to talk like he was young, and I blamed Harmony for that.

"What deal is that?" I questioned.

My father was never the one to talk to me in detail about his lifestyle. He figured the less I knew, the better, but I actually thought the total opposite. The more I knew, the better prepared I'd be.

"Business is expanding, which is always a good thing. As a matter of fact, we have a huge announcement to make at dinner…which reminds me," my father said, holding up his index finger. He grabbed the walkie-talkie that was on his desk and spoke into it. "Maria," he called out to one of his workers.

"Yes, sir!" she replied in a heavy Spanish accent.

"We are having a dinner guest tonight, so make sure you set an extra plate," he instructed.

"Sure thing," she replied before they ended their communication.

"Dinner guest? In the house? Well, that's a first," I continued, picking up exactly where I'd left off.

"Yeah, you know how private I am. Trust is something that's earned," he preached.

"So, I take it this is a person you trust?" I asked.

"Why else would he be coming to dinner?"

We spent the next twenty minutes listening to Harmony bring my father up to speed on what had been going on in her life. She also put her bid in for a trip to Disney World, and considering how much my parents spoiled her, I knew that was where we were headed. Just as we were walking out the office, the doorbell rang, and Maria rushed to get it. By the time we made it to the dining area, Courtney had come through the door.

"Uncle Willie!" she said, laughing and greeting my father with a hug.

My dad laughed too before the four of us headed towards the table.

"Aye, Princess, yo' nose getting fat as fuck," Courtney whispered to me before taking the seat across from me.

Instead of responding, I rolled my eyes, which I was sure she caught on to, but knowing Courtney, she couldn't care less. We sat at the table and waited for my mother, Uncle Quintin and Auntie Domo to join us. Courtney and my dad talked more about the trip to Cuba while I looked in my phone. I thought about texting JA because I had blown him and his apology off, but I figured, if anything, he should be reaching out to me, so I quickly dismissed that idea. After stalking The Shade Room's page on Instagram, I jumped on Snapchat and did the same thing. About three minutes later, I heard my uncle and auntie come in the front door. My dad got up and went into the living room area with them, and a few seconds later, I heard a bunch of laughter as they made their way back to where we were seated.

"I hope you like soul food. You know how you Puerto Rican niggaz are," I heard my dad say.

"Ahhhh, come on now. You know I ain't Puerto Rican, old man."

I immediately froze when I heard that voice. I had to be tweaking because there was no way in the world JA was inside my parents' house. Before I could turn around and confirm that I wasn't in the twilight zone, my dad said my name.

"Aye, Princess, this is JA. JA, this is my daughter, Princess," he said, introducing us.

The look on JA's face was one for the ages. He looked surprised, upset, and confused all in one.

"Hey, how you doing?" I said, forcing a fake smile, trying my hardest to avoid eye contact.

"I'm straight, shorty, how are you?" he asked with a devilish grin.

"Good," I replied, looking away.

My eyes landed on Harmony and Courtney, and both of their mouths were wide open. I discreetly placed my index finger to my lips, signaling them to hush, and thank God, they did.

"A'ight, JA, you can take that seat right next to Princess… Oh, and this is my granddaughter, Harmony and my niece, Courtney," my father stated.

The three of them waved to each other before he took the seat next to me. Just then, my mom walked into the dining area, and the dinner party was complete. She looked around the table before locking eyes with me and smiling. Well, I thought she was smiling at me until she spoke.

"Is that my boy down there?" she said, walking around the table towards where JA and I were sitting.

JA stood and gave my mom a hug, and that was the icing on the cake for me.

Once she sat down, the kitchen crew brought the food out, and everyone dug in. The tension was so thick in the room between JA, Harmony, Courtney and I, while my parents, auntie and uncle sat there unbothered. I couldn't believe this shit. I wondered how much his ass had been lying about. My right leg began to shake under the table, and I was ready for this shit to be over with so I could get all the answers I needed. After we were done eating dessert, I began to get up from the table when my father stopped me.

"Hold on, baby girl, I got an announcement to make," my father stated.

I let out a low sigh before sitting back down. Once my ass was planted in the cushioned seat, he began to speak.

"So, I'm going to keep this short… Harmony, go upstairs, baby," he instructed.

Harmony got up and did as she was told, and once she was out of sight, my father began to speak again.

"There's no secret that my brother and I run a very lucrative business, and we have been blessed to be successful and rich in all of what we do. However, you may not have noticed, but we are getting old," my father paused, and my uncle picked up.

"So, with that being said, we can't run shit how we used to anymore. We not giving it up, but we are passing along the main duties to JA."

Once those words left my uncle's mouth, I began to choke. All eyes landed on me while Courtney laughed.

"I'm so sorry, continue," I said, apologizing.

"We've raised JA like he's our son. His father was our right-hand man, and when he was killed, we took him in and made sure him and Janice was straight. Eventually, JA started doing business with us, and he's the only person in our organization that we can fully trust, with no questions asked. Now, we not stepping down, but he will handle all of the organization's operations from here on out," my father announced.

"Damn, straight up! Congratulations, JA," Courtney stated.

"Yeah, that's what's up. I don't know you, JA, but you have to be a stand-up guy for my father to do something like this," I added.

"Thanks, y'all, and I'ma show y'all that y'all made the right decision," JA stated.

"Oh, we not worried about that. We gon' hold a meeting in about two weeks, letting the entire organization know what's going on," my dad replied, standing.

The rest of the table followed his lead and headed towards the living room. I began to walk out but felt someone grab me by the tail of my shirt. I turned around and locked eyes with JA.

"We need to talk," he said in a subtle tone.

"Talk about what?" I snapped.

"Man, chill out, we got a lot to talk about," he assured me.

"No the fuck we don't. You are a fucking liar. This whole time, you got me thinking that you this wholesome-ass businessman when it's the total opposite. Like, nigga, you even lied about your pops and the way he died!" I yelled.

At this point, I didn't give a fuck who heard me. The shit had already hit the fan, and we were all grown. I needed JA to feel my wrath.

"Wait, so all this my fault? I'm the only one who lied?" he asked, still calm and relaxed.

"We not talking about me, we talking about you and yo' lying ass," I said, mushing him in the face with my index finger.

JA laughed, which only made matters worse. I crossed my arms over my chest and waited to find out what the fuck was so funny.

"You know what, fuck you, JA!" I said, walking off, but I didn't make it far before he grabbed me again.

"Look, baby, let's go somewhere where we can talk," he pleaded with me.

"AGAIN, TALK ABOUT WHAT?" I yelled even louder this time.

Courtney walked back into the dining room where we were with a confused look on her face.

"Aye, y'all loud as fuck," she stated.

I turned to my cousin and said, "I don't give a fuck who hears me. I'm sick of all this shit."

I could tell by the look on JA's face that he was getting pissed off, and that was what I wanted to happen. I wanted him to feel exactly how I felt.

"Courtney, I guess she wanna put on a show," JA replied.

"Yeah, you right, I do. Let's put on a show. As a matter fact, a circus since you a fuckin' clown anyway," I snapped.

JA's face turned red, and I knew I had hit the right buttons. He took his right hand and rubbed it across his beard before taking a seat on the edge of the table.

"Seriously, Princess, y'all need to take this shit down to your house," Courtney interjected.

"House? Awwww, the one that's getting renovated?" JA added.

"Fuck you," I hissed.

"Y'all both STOP!" Courtney intervened.

"Nah, Princess wanna put on a show, let's put on a motherfucking show. Come on," he said, grabbing me by my arm, pulling me into the living room where everybody was seated.

JA

I led her by the hand into the living room where her parents, aunt and uncle were taking shots. Everyone paused when they noticed us holding hands, but before anyone could say anything, I spoke up first.

"Aye, Quincy, how many years it took you to finish medical school? And Meka, how about law school? Did you pass the bar on your first try?" I asked, directing my questions to Princess' parents.

Everyone in the room looked confused, so I continued. "I just wanna know since you a doctor, Q, and Meka, you a lawyer."

Princess snatched her arm away, but I grabbed it again, this time with a much tighter grip.

"Boy, are you drunk? Why the fuck y'all holding hands? Did I miss something?" Quincy asked.

"Aye, peep game. I met this shorty almost a year ago, and I can't lie, I fell for her hard. I mean, she was perfect, y'all, everything I ever wanted in a woman. Shorty was so right, I cut off all my hoes just to be faithful to her because I could never imagine hurting her. The thing was, though, she told me that her parents was some stuck-up rich motherfuckers, so I automatically assumed that they'd frown their nose up at a street nigga like me, so I lied. I lied and told her that I was a businessman. Well, technically, I didn't lie now that I think about it because I do own several businesses. I guess I'll say that I didn't tell her the whole truth about me. She knew nothing about the street me, but how I was brought up, that's some shit you don't tell people all willy-nilly anyway. So, long story short, she found out about the real me, and now I'm guessing she wanna bounce," I said, pausing briefly and looking at Princess.

"If she loves you, then why she wanna bounce?" Princess' mom asked.

"If you love me, then why you wanna bounce, Princess?" I turned to her and asked.

Everyone's mouths dropped in the room, including Courtney, and she knew what was going on already. Silence fell upon everyone as we all looked around the room, staring at each other.

"Wait. Wait. Wait. Wait. Princess and JA, y'all knew each other prior to today?" Quincy asked.

"Yup, but I didn't know she was your daughter until today," I admitted truthfully.

"This shit is crazy! I don't even know what to say," Princess' mother stated, sitting on the arm of the couch next to her husband.

"Oh, and since we coming clean, Princess, you wanna tell them, or should I?" I questioned.

"JA, you bet' not. Come on, we need to talk," she replied, pulling me towards the door.

"Nah, you wanted to do this shit right here in the open, right?" I replied, yanking away from her.

"BOTH OF YALL STOP! I'm as shocked as the next person, but y'all grown and y'all need to handle this shit like adults. I commend both of you for not running y'all mouth because essentially, both of you was protecting your family. JA, I love you like a son, and if I had to choose a man for her, it would be you. And Princess, I know for a fact that you have a good nigga in JA cuz I practically raised him myself. What I need y'all to do is go down the street and take care of this," Quincy stood and stated.

I looked over at Princess, who had tears in her eyes. I hated to see her cry, and it was fucked up that things had played out this way, but they had. I was starting to feel bad about my part in the whole ordeal. If I had just been honest from the beginning, none of this shit would have taken place. I turned to Princess to talk to her, but she was already storming out the front door. I didn't hesitate to run after her, catching her as she powerwalked down the street.

"Would you just stop and listen?" I asked, jumping in front of her, blocking her way.

"Listen to what? You lied to me," she cried.

"And you lied to me, too. One lie doesn't trump the others, we was both wrong," I said, trying to reason with her.

"Look, JA, I love you with all my heart, but I need time—"

"Time for what?" I asked, cutting her off.

"I need time to think. All this shit today has been too much for me."

"Let me get this straight. You mad because I lied about the same shit you lied about? You sound fucking stupid!" I yelled.

"And you are fucking stupid. Look, leave me the fuck alone. I don't want to have shit to do with you," she said, staring at me straight in the eyes.

"I don't see how that's possible and you got my babies in there," I replied, trying a much calmer approach now.

"Yo' babies, huh? TSK! I got a few more months before they get here, until then, I'm good on you," she smirked, walking around me and towards her house.

"A'ight, bet. Remember this what you wanted."

Princess acknowledged my words by sticking up her middle finger, never once looking back. I was beyond frustrated at this point. Yeah, I loved her, but kissing her ass was not a part of my plans, especially when we were both equally at fault. I walked back down to Quincy's house. I thought about going in and apologizing for how everything had played out, but I couldn't. I knew that they were going to have more questions and that was some shit I didn't feel like talking about at the moment.

I hopped in my ride and headed back towards the city. I wanted to be with Princess and be a family more than anything in this world, but my pride would not allow me to kiss her ass in order to have that. She had clearly stated that she didn't want shit to do with me, and I planned on granting her wish. I just hoped this didn't get in the way of being in my boys' life.

PRINCESS

Two weeks had passed since the blow up at dinner, and I hadn't been out much. Courtney was taking care of everything business-wise, and Harmony was out for her two-week break, so I pretty much never left the house. Because I was carrying twins, I was required to see the doctor once a week now, and it killed me going to those appointments alone. I hadn't heard from JA at all, which really shocked me. I thought that maybe he would reach out to me at least once, but he hadn't even done that. My emotions were all over the place, and I cried at least six times a day. I missed him so much, and the fact that he hadn't even checked on me or the twins was eating away at me. I knew JA was a prideful man, but I thought I had some type of weird power over him that caused his pride to shrink a little, but I was wrong.

"Ms. Taylor, you are all set. Your next appointment is next Thursday at two o'clock."

Hearing the nurse's voice broke me out of my trance. I got up and headed to the desk, grabbing the card out of her hand that contained all the information for my next appointment. I thanked her and told Harmony I was ready to go. I promised her that we would do lunch at the Sugar Shack after I left here, so that was where we were headed. After driving about thirty minutes, I lucked up on a parking spot by the front door. Regardless of the day or time, this place was always crowded for no reason. The drinks and food were overrated, and the shit was extremely overpriced, but it was Harmony's day to choose, so I just took one for the team.

We waited five minutes before we were seated. The only good thing about this place was that their service was rather prompt, and the staff was always friendly. After snuggling up in a small booth with my favorite girl, we both looked over the menu, trying to decide what we wanted.

"Ma, why are you frowning?" Harmony looked up at me and asked.

"Baby, I know you love these booths, but it's uncomfortable for me," I replied, rubbing my stomach.

"Oh snap, mommy, I didn't think of that," she said. "Excuse me, ma'am," Harmony said, flagging the waitress down. "Can we please move because this booth is uncomfortable for my mother," she continued.

The pretty, young waitress looked at us and smiled, and I shook my head.

"No problem, princess, you and Mommy can follow me this way," she said, grabbing the waters and menus off the table and taking them with her.

We walked a few feet over to a table not far from the window.

"While I'm here, can I take you guys' order?" she asked, grabbing a notepad from her apron pocket.

Harmony ordered for us, getting me a cheeseburger, well done with extra pickles, while she ordered chicken tenders and cheese fries for herself. After we wrapped things up with the waitress, I turned to Harmony.

"Soooo, somebody's birthday is coming up soon," I stated, smiling.

"Yes, mommy. I'm about to be the BIG ELEVEN!" she replied excitedly.

"I know, honey, what do you want to do?" I asked.

I regretted asking that question as soon as those words left my lips. Harmony rambled on and on for about ten minutes about this extravagant party she wanted to have. This damn girl didn't want a normal kid party, she wanted a diamonds and pearls theme. She even had the audacity to ask if she could give out small diamond bracelets to her guests as parting gifts. I had never been so happy to see food in my life when they brought ours out. Hopefully, that would make her shut up.

"I'm about to go to the bathroom, you good?" I asked, scooting my chair back.

"Yea, Ma, I went before we left the doctor's office, and so did you," she giggled.

"Girl, shut up. I'll be back, and don't move," I warned.

I headed towards the back where the restroom was located. I went inside and grabbed the first available stall, which was the handicapped one. It worked out for me since I had all this extra weight and I needed extra room. After relieving myself, I went to the sink and washed my hands. I grabbed a few sheets of paper towel and dried off my hands while staring in the mirror.

"Oh my God, you look so pretty pregnant," a woman said, exiting the stall and joining me at the sink.

"Thank you," I replied, giving off a friendly smile.

"You're welcome. You are carrying it very well," she said, leaving out before me.

I stared at myself a little longer before tossing the paper towels in the trash, leaving one in my hand to open the door with. As soon as I stepped out, I turned the corner, heading back to the table, but not before colliding with someone.

"I'm sorr—"

I stopped mid-sentence as I stood face to face with JA. Instantly, tears began to cloud my vision, but I tried my hardest to hold them back.

"How y'all doing?" he asked, rubbing my stomach.

"We good," I replied, taking off, attempting to walk around him, but he grabbed me.

"Princess, how long we gon' keep this up?" he questioned.

"How long is forever?" I shot back.

"A'ight," was all he said before walking off.

"JA, WAIT!" I yelled.

He slowly turned around and waited as if he wanted me to say something else.

"I made six months today," I said, looking down at the ground.

"I know, ya moms told me," he laughed, walking back over to where I was standing.

"My mommy, really?"

"Yeah, ever since she found out you were pregnant, she's been keeping me posted," he informed me.

"I can't believe they knew all this time, thanks to Harmony's talkative ass," I said, letting out a soft chuckle.

"I could have told you that, her ass can't hold water," JA replied, walking closer, invading my personal space.

"Speaking of Harmony, where she at? I miss my daughter," he grinned, and I suddenly got wet.

"She's at the table. Who you here with?"

Before he could answer, the female who complimented me in the bathroom walked up, locking her arm with his.

"Baby, our table is ready," she gushed.

You ever feel like your heart was ripped from your chest and squeezed until all the blood was drained out of it? That was the only way to describe how I felt at this very moment. JA must have noticed the hurt in my eyes because he smoothly removed his arm from hers.

"It was nice seeing you again," I said, forcing a fake smile and walking away.

I could hear him calling out to me, but my body was numb; I couldn't turn around if I wanted to.

"Harmony, let's go!" I said, approaching the table.

"But, mommy, you haven't even eaten yet and—"

"HARMONY, I SAID LET'S GO!" I yelled this time, causing her to jump.

Harmony got up from the table with the saddest look on her face I had ever seen. I reached into my purse, pulled out a hundred-dollar bill and threw it on the table before walking out. I was happy I had parked close, so that meant I didn't have to walk long, which meant I didn't have to hold back these tears much longer. Once inside the car, I looked over at my daughter and felt bad. She hadn't done anything to me, yet I was taking my anger out on her.

"I'm sorry, baby, Mommy just dealing with some shit. I'll tell you about it on the ride home. We just needed to get out of there quick," I explained.

"It's OK, mommy. I know the pregnancy is taking a toll on you," she replied, giving me a warm smile.

Hearing her say that made me feel much better. I cranked up the car and prepared to pull out of the parking spot when Harmony yelled, "OH MY GOD, MOMMY, THERE GO THAT MAN AGAIN!"

"What man, baby?" I wondered as I searched for who she was referring to.

"Him right there in that black jacket. Mommy, it's like I see him everywhere I go. He's at my school every day but never picks up any kids. The other day when I went with Courtney, he magically appeared there, too. Mommy, I'm scared of him." My daughter began to cry.

I put the car in park and searched for the mysterious man but still didn't see him.

"He's walking over here towards the car, Ma!" Harmony screamed, locking the car doors.

I looked over at her, and then in the direction she was pointing in. My heart dropped as I laid eyes on a ghost. The man I stared at was none other than Pierre, her DEAD father.

HALFTIME

CPSIA information can be obtained
at www.ICGtesting.com
Printed in the USA
LVHW05s1944200618
581394LV00021B/401/P